THE HAND
OF PETRARCH

AND

OTHER STORIES

BY

T. R. SULLIVAN

TOUT BIEN OU RIEN

BOSTON AND NEW YORK
HOUGHTON MIFFLIN COMPANY
THE RIVERSIDE PRESS

1913

TO MY WIFE

Contents

THE HAND OF PETRARCH

THE HAND OF PETRARCH

I

MESSER ENRICO CAPRA, the goldsmith of Bergamo, was in the year
1374, as certain veracious chroniclers of his
day instruct us, a famous man, justly admired
and respected through all the neighboring
country-side. His reputation for good work-
manship had extended, on the one hand, far up
the valleys of the Brembo and the Serio, those
tributaries of the River Adda which encircle
his native stronghold; and, on the other, it
had travelled eastward at least as far as Bres-
cia, where a fine crucifix from his hand stood
in the old cathedral. If his name and fame
had not spread abroad over the Lombard
plain to its great capital of Milan, and thence,
with ever-widening vibrations to the horizon's
verge, why, that, according to his fellow
citizens, was entirely his own fault. For,
while they could praise without reserve the
excelling art which had brought him ease and

wealth in middle life, they were compelled, with the same breath, to deplore its abrupt, ineffectual end. He had chosen to hide his talent in the earth at the moment of its perfection. And that, unhappily, was long ago; for fifteen years and more this talent had proved unfruitful. In art, not to produce incessantly is to cease to exist; and Messer Enrico Capra, at the age of sixty-three, still vigorous, intelligent, and lovable, had become, so far as art recognized him, a creature of the past; for present shortcomings, irresistibly compared by his friends and kindred to the unprofitable servant who was cast into outer darkness at the divine command.

Though he had remained a bachelor and lived alone, except for a houseful of servants, there was little of the recluse about him. The house stood upon a narrow street near the workshop, which had passed long since into other hands; outwardly, it was a modest abode, unadorned and unpretentious; within, it showed no lack of comfort. At the back, a sunny little garden, sloping to the southwest near an angle of the bastions, had a wide prospect over hill and plain; so wide that the

guests, who were often entertained there un-
ceremoniously, but sufficiently, could discern
on a clear day the towers of three cities —
Monza, Treviglio, and Milan. It was the last,
undoubtedly, which suggested a byword, first
whispered amongst these few, to pass current
afterward in the town — the byword, namely,
that Messer Enrico, the famous goldsmith,
could walk in his own garden and look beyond his fame.

Messer Enrico, himself, hardly knew how
often he had looked beyond it to those same
distant towers of the Lombard capital. For
beneath them had once lived for many years
the man who, unwittingly at first, then despite
his own urgent remonstrance, had been the
sole cause of the goldsmith's strange cessation
from artistic labor; the man who was the
foremost scholar of his time, the leader of
thought so distinguished that he burst all
bonds of hampering tradition and freed the
world of letters from the shackles of theo-
logy; no less a man than the great Petrarch
— poet, philosopher, and historian, friend
and counsellor of princes, hermit of Vaucluse
and Arquà, sage of Venice and Padua, as well

as of Milan, where, humblest if not least among his admirers, the worthy goldsmith of Bergamo was first admitted to his presence.

That the establishment of a personal relation with the master should have been to this devotee a difficult task is not surprising. The age was marked by a genuine interest in literature ; Dante had but lately died, and Boccaccio's star had risen. Between the two shone Petrarch, whose transcendent lustre constituted him the supreme arbiter, to whom all literary craftsmen of any pretension appealed as a matter of course. And these competitors for the laurel were innumerable, even as the sands of the sea. For it was not only an age of great promise and performance, but also one of futile attempt and deadly imitation. The mania of authorship had grown into a malignant disorder, from which there seemed to be no immunity for high or low. Statesmen, senators, journey-men, shopkeepers, nay, even apprentices were affected by it; a plague more terrible than that of Florence, it threatened to lay waste the land. While amid it all, overburdened with greatness, the dominant spirit, indirectly respons-

ible for the infliction, found himself besieged
in his house and set upon at every street-cor-
ner by the callow wits that longed to soar
and prayed for support. Until at last, goaded
beyond his patience, he barred his door against
all clamorous invasion.

It was by gentle means alone that Messer
Enrico Capra sought to attain what force
could not accomplish. Through subtle compliment and quaint device he aroused the
great man's curiosity, impressing upon him
the profound sincerity of his devotion. He
collected rare copies of the master, whose
portrait, arms, and name in golden letters
everywhere adorned the walls of his house
at Bergamo. By degrees the house became
a shrine where, day by day, he burned incense before his idol. Unlike the ignoble
herd, he had no productive aspirations of his
own to further, no manuscripts to offer in
evidence of latent genius. If he gradually
neglected his honorable calling to the point
of its final abandonment, he did so merely
for purposes of study, that he might gain
thus a better understanding of the product
from the master - hand. At that hand, he,

himself, asked nothing, expected nothing. His one ardent hope was to prove worthy of Petrarch's friendship, if, by some fortunate accident, it should ever be accorded him.

After years of waiting a day arrived when his patient zeal was rewarded. A local magistrate brought him word, with all the deference which so great an occasion demanded, that the noble Petrarch, the illustrious, the laurel-crowned, would receive Messer Enrico Capra, of Bergamo, whenever it should please him to present himself; furthermore, that, desiring to verify the good repute of so faithful an admirer, he prayed that the visit might not be long deferred. Overjoyed, the goldsmith posted to Milan, where, trembling with exultation, he met Petrarch face to face, at last, and was welcomed with a benignant cordiality which almost turned his brain. Life for him, he declared, should be henceforth one long consecration to the noblest incentive that he had ever known. The master smiled at an infatuation which by many an argument he conscientiously strove to overcome; the scholar's labors, he urged, were exacting, and Messer Enrico was no longer of an age to assume them; while, as an artist, new triumphs, well worth winning, no doubt awaited him. But to such counsel the self-constituted disciple refused to listen. His art was a bygone thing; he had forsaken all it promised for one high, illuminating purpose, fixed as the stars in their courses. Thus opposed, the leader, touched against his will by homage that he could not control, suffered himself to be led, and protested no more.

Thereafter, though the two seldom met, their friendly intercourse was maintained by active correspondence. Petrarch had a weakness for letter-writing; and the indefatigable student's appeals for advice or sympathy were never left unheeded. Now, it was the text of some obscure passage upon which he craved enlightenment; now, he had acquired some *editio princeps*, or some new memorial of his patron, to whom the happy circumstance must be communicated. On rare occasions he reappeared in Milan for a day, that became a festal one. So, carefully tended, the flame upon the altar was kept alive, and the idol fostered it. Yet for a long time one last

concession was withheld. Over and over again
the goldsmith implored him to bestow upon
Bergamo a day, an hour of his gracious presence. The master smiled and shook his head;
only to yield in the end, worn out, as he,
himself, has recorded, by incessant importun-
ities. Once more Messer Enrico made his
familiar journey to the capital. But this time
he journeyed back with Petrarch, and at the
gates of Bergamo all the great ones of the
city awaited his return.

That memorable visit occurred in the autumn of the year 1359. And, duly impressed
with its importance, Petrarch took pains to
describe it shortly afterward in detail. From
his own pen we learn how the Podestà and
the dignitaries flung wide their palace-doors,
disputing for his entertainment; how the
poor goldsmith trembled lest his humble roof
should be forsaken for some nobler lodging;
how his reverence denied them all, and, descending at Messer Enrico's house, delighted
in its treasures; how, after a royal banquet,
he slept upon a purple couch, surrounded
by the choicest books, in a chamber glitter-
ing with gold, where none had slept before,

and none ever should sleep again; finally, how, on the following day, he departed, oppressed with honors, escorted by the city fathers; and taking leave of his infatuated host, when the homeward journey was half over, actually feared that the good man might lose his reason, or die from excess of joy. But, on the contrary, since that eventful day of long ago, it could truly be said that Messer Enrico Capra had lived upon its recollection.

Into the master's life, however, time and circumstance brought many a change. The cares of Petrarch multiplied; he became involved in state affairs, was sent abroad to one foreign court after another upon diplomatic missions. To years of enforced wandering succeeded years of restlessness; he removed from Milan to Venice, thence to Padua, where age came upon him suddenly; and, in declining health, he made still another move — the final one. Twelve miles away, at Arquà, in the Euganean Hills, he built an ideal hermitage. There, amid his books and flowers, the closing years of his life were passed in perfect peace. Until his last hour the scholarly pursuits which he loved best never ceased to interest him. His motto was the text from Ecclesiasticus : " When a man hath done, then he beginneth ; and when he leaveth off, then he shall be doubtful." Yet if, now and then, some remote rumor of the world penetrated to his quiet sanctuary, it brought him no disturbance. Upon the world's distractions he had turned his back forever.

Time, dealing thus with the master, wrought upon the disciple likewise its inevitable changes. For many years Messer Enrico's stream of life flowed calmly on with few reënforcements from the fountain-head. After Petrarch's departure from Milan, the goldsmith never looked upon his face again. Gradually even the correspondence languished, coming at last with a perceptible shade of bitterness to its end. For this some fault justly might have been alleged on both sides, yet its direct cause was the goldsmith's persistent endeavor to gain a boon which had never been absolutely denied him. He had long desired to possess a copy of Petrarch's Italian verses, prepared by the master's own hand. In the series of sonnets, so graceful, so melodious, of which unrequited love for Laura

forms the theme, Messer Enrico found the
highest expression of his idol's genius; and
the world has confirmed that judgment in
manifold editions of the little book, proclaimed incomparable. But in the eyes of
its author, it was a youthful trifle, crude,
immature, almost unworthy of preservation.
While, therefore, he refrained from dismissing the goldsmith's request for the manuscript with a blunt refusal, and even con-
sented to make the copy, he did not conceal
the fact that his compliance was a reluctant
one. With the procrastination which developed in his later life, he postponed the labor
of love from day to day, from week to week,
from year to year. In the mean time, relying
upon the half-hearted assurance, Messer Enrico devoted himself to preparing a recept-
acle worthy of what would prove his richest
treasure. He designed a golden casket, so
splendid that its counterpart had never been
imagined. It was adorned with reliefs illus-
trating the sonnets, the life and death of
Laura; and these were upheld by groups of
figures drawn from the argument of the im-
mortal poem, wherein Death triumphed over

Love, Fame over Death, Time over Fame, and Eternity over all. This, when finished, should be another wonder of the world, and the goldsmith, resuming the art he had long neglected, brought all his skill to bear upon it. Petrarch, duly advised of the scheme, at first professed keen interest. He renewed his promise, and began his copy of the manuscript; but the interest waned, the work was delayed, cast aside; and fulfilment of the promise seemed farther off than ever when the goldsmith's own work on the wondrous casket drew near its end. Word reached him of his master's removal to Arquà, whither he sent an appeal, pathetically urgent. No answer came. The setting upon which he had toiled for years in secret had received its final touches, yet it still lacked the precious jewel. The good goldsmith was human; waiting vainly, he sometimes permitted his vexation to break forth in sharp reproaches; but these were always followed by a mood of repentance wherein he framed excuses for this cruel neglect which time must surely justify. After twenty years of blind faith, one journeys backward slowly to the point of recantation.

The casket, wrapped in cloth of gold, was
hidden away in the richly furnished chamber, devoted to memorials of the master,
which Messer Enrico revisited alone at long
intervals. One brilliant day in spring he unlocked the door again, unbarred the shutters,
flooded the room with light. The sunshine
streamed upon its golden walls, playing about
the heap of ashes on the hearth, touching
lightly one half-burned brand there, which,
alas! would never be rekindled. Opposite,
on a small table at the bedside, lay a pile of
books, just as the beloved hand had left them,
long ago. They were buried in dust, but, at the
risk of disturbing their arrangement, Messer
Enrico would not brush away a grain of it.
Sighing, he made his round, as he had often
done before; and then, returning to the table,
looked down at it in silence. The room was
still as death; its windows opened upon the
garden, and from without came only a murmur of the rose - leaves, with the call of a
blackbird growing fainter in the distance.
These were sounds too slight to hear. But,
suddenly, a nearer and sharper sound behind
him interrupted his reverie. He turned, with

a start, to find that the only intruder was the
playful breeze which, scattering the ash-heap,
had tumbled the charred stick down upon the
hearthstone and broken it. But, in turning,
he caught his robe upon a corner of the table;
a book slipped off, opening as it fell; and a
loose bit of parchment fluttered out between
the leaves. He picked this up, perceiving, to
his surprise, some lines of verse written upon
it, in Petrarch's own handwriting. They were
incomplete and blurred by corrections, breaking off in the middle of a phrase; but they
were addressed "To My Good Friend, Messer
Enrico Capra," whose eyes now filled with
tears as he tried to read them. He soon discovered that he had lighted, by chance, upon
an unfinished sonnet in which the master had
intended to express sympathy with his court-
eous host and to do him honor. The intention had never been carried out; yet the
kindly thought was there in this rough draft,
and its discovery touched Messer Enrico
deeply. All the force of his affection revived
at once. Before the day was done he had despatched to Arquà an account of his little adventure and its effect upon him, without even

a reference to the unfulfilled obligation, or any note whatsoever of complaint. To omit all mention of his bitter disappointment at this time was to make a strong entreaty, as he well knew; and the master, reading between the lines of the letter, so understood it. His prompt reply was a prayer for tolerance. "Kind and devoted friend," he wrote, "thou art of all men the gentlest, the most forgiving. Know, then, that my broken covenant with thee is to me a weight of sorrow. Let thy indulgence absolve me. I have declined into the autumn of my years; but ere this year's harvest is fully garnered, the covenant shall be redeemed. To this I pledge my hand."

With infinite joy Messer Enrico returned thanks for the remorseful acknowledgment, and resigned himself again to patient waiting. Spring passed; midsummer came; the vintage would be an early one, they said, though it was still far off. He watched for that, noting each day the season's progress, smiling at the petty hopes of gain, so dear to his neighbors. And when evening fell, he strolled alone upon the city walls through the lengthening shadows, not to take delight in the sunset, but to look eastward over the plain. This habit grew, until his fellow townsmen regarded it with wonder; and when he lingered at his favorite angle of the rampart, they shrugged their shoulders, whispering: "There is Messer Enrico on the watch again! What does he find to see, that we do not? What messenger is he expecting?"

One July evening of the year 1374, as he stood musing in his wonted place, his attention was suddenly arrested by a strange excitement in the lower town. Along one of its narrow streets groups of men were forming to discuss some question eagerly. The news, whatever it was, spread from the door of one wine-shop to another, handed on with emphatic gestures. All this stir provoked him to inquiry. He hurried down the nearest flight of steps into the gloom of a vaulted passage, leading out below the walls. There, in the dark, he met the dreadful word. Petrarch was dead! Stunned by the shock, as if a savage hand had struck him, he stumbled on, tracing the word to its source with incoherent questions, until he confirmed the news beyond a doubt. His noble master had died ten days before at Arquà, quietly, without pain, falling asleep in his chair, among his books, alone. This became clear, and at this point all struggle ceased. Nothing else was clear for a long time.

II

Six weeks later Messer Enrico came to himself, and was informed by Marcello, his faithful servant, that he had been desperately ill of a fever, wavering between life and death. When he learned the duration of his illness, his mind reverted at once to the vanishing point, and he brooded, in silence, upon the insupportable sorrow. An hour afterward he roused himself to ask, abruptly, if nothing in all these days and weeks had come from Arquà. Was there no letter? no message? In anxiety that he could not comprehend, his attendant, with a negative sign, entreated him to sleep. Not until his convalescence was it explained to him that this question, many times repeated, had been the haunting theme of his delirium.

It haunted him still, though he was careful not to betray himself. Had nothing come from Arquà? No—nothing, nothing. Yet something would come, surely. To that hope he clung with obstinate persistence. Had he not his master's word for it? Would not that hold good, even though the master were in his grave?

The cool, bright days of autumn restored him to his little world. He was a well man, now, he said. But others could perceive, though he did not, the ineffaceable signs of his long illness; in its course he had passed from vigor to old age. Health and strength might still be his, yet with a difference; it was clear that he must refrain from overtaxing them. Of this limitation, however, he seemed quite unconscious, when he walked and talked among his neighbors, planning a little journey that should give him necessary change to set the seal upon his recovery — a journey to Padua and Venice, as he took care to state. Thus, by slow degrees, he warned them of his departure. And thus they heard, one day, without surprise, the news that he was gone.

Disregarding all advice to the contrary, he

set forth entirely alone. But though his steps turned toward the east, neither to Padua nor Venice did he direct them. His goal of pilgrimage, so cautiously defended from cold indifference or idle jest, was Arquà only — Arquà, the simple mountain village — Arquà Petrarca, coupled forevermore with the dead master's name. Journeying by easy stages, he turned at Este from the Paduan highway, and struck off into the hills. Through the haze of a fine October afternoon, he climbed the last slope, over a rough road that ended in a group of houses irregularly placed about the open square, dusty and grass-grown, which formed the nucleus of the little town. At one side stood the inn, denoted only by a withered branch above its door; and across the farther end stretched the long, low wall of a church, severe in line, without adornment. From its tower the call to vespers rang insistently, as if to hasten the steps of certain loiterers drawn tardily to the office; but that summons was not sharp enough; for while the stranger paused to look about him, a beadle enforced it sternly, driving the stragglers in like sheep. Messer Enrico was moved piously to follow them. But, as he crossed the square, his purpose changed; he stopped with a cry, kneeling then and there in the dust, at sight of the line carved upon a quaint monument which stood near the church-door in the shadow of the wall.

Frigida Francisci lapis hic tegit ossa Petrarce! This, then, was the master's tomb! This rude sarcophagus of red marble, raised upon four short columns above the level of vulgar life, to dignify the barren place and be its glory and its ornament till time should cease and earthly honor sweep into oblivion! The poor townsmen and their parish officer had passed it by, carelessly; they dispersed as they assembled, with slow indifference, while the stranger watched them from his window at the inn, whither he had turned for lodging. This, though the best which the town afforded, was of so primitive a sort that the host mumbled profuse apologies for its deficiencies; but the window overlooked the square, and to Messer Enrico all the rest mattered nothing. Through his eager questions the man soon gained confidence, and chattered freely. Oh, yes, he had seen the master sometimes — after death, had looked upon his face; all the arts and essences of the East had been applied to its preservation, leaving it wonderfully lifelike. Everybody in the village, old or young, had followed the body to the tomb yonder; there had been garlands and banners, acolytes and incense, the cardinal himself—a splendid funeral, truly a nine days' wonder! Had the signore visited the good man's house? By leaning forward and turning the head to the right, one could see its tiled roof— there, higher up the hill, out of the town. It was worth the climb, if only to get the prospect from its garden.

Messer Enrico smiled at these last words, as he toiled in the sunset up the stony path to the garden-gate, through which he looked, with a full heart, along a trim walk leading to the doorway of the house. The rusty chain rattled as he pulled it, stirring the bell within. And, at the sound, from a low ilex-tree in the garden a startled bird flew, twittering up into the clear sky. Then the house-door opened, and a man, white-haired, infirm, of very gentle bearing, came slowly down the walk to admit the visitor at the first hint of his errand.

"Welcome, signore, in my master's name.

Alas, that it should be too late for such a word from his own lips!"

"It is the grievous counterstroke of fortune; for I am one who loved him — Capra, Enrico Capra, the goldsmith of Bergamo. And thou wert of his household?"

"His body-servant, Vitale, signore. It was I who found him in his armchair, sleeping, never to wake again. I remain for a time in charge of the place. Will it please the signore to come in?"

His voice failed him. Silently, he led the way up an outer staircase, through the arched loggia, to the main floor of the house — a series of small rooms, opening one into another, bright and cheerful, with the comfortable air that is derived from daily use. There was the poet's chamber; here the chair in which he had fallen asleep; this was his library, and these closed cabinets contained the precious books, deeded long ago to Venice, but entrusted for delivery to his friend and patron, the Lord of Padua, who had placed his seal upon them all; all, save one, that volume of Cicero, with which the master was occupied at the moment of his death. It still lay upon the floor, where it had dropped from his lifeless hand. The old man indicated these things in a whispered word or two, while the stranger followed him with tear-dimmed eyes. Then they passed out together upon an iron balcony overhanging a wide, green valley, which opened toward the western plain. There were vineyards and olive orchards upon all the slopes; above them, from the rocky heights stretching eastward, clumps of pine-trees stood out against the sky. Here, where the master loved to sit, they lingered, leaning upon the rail, while day's colors deepened, and the lovely landscape grew lovelier in the afterglow. The bitterness of grief abated with these quiet influences, until speech no longer was impossible. Messer Enrico, producing his last letter from the poet, explained the nature of the bond to which it bore witness, and sought further evidence regarding it. To his discomfiture this proved inconclusive. It appeared that the master, shortly before his death, had burned in his brasier a heap of old papers; but what these were, and why he had chosen to destroy them, it was idle to conjecture. Of their import the servant could say nothing; and the sealed cabinets, he was sure, contained only books. Were there no other papers, then? None, so far as he knew. If any such had escaped the brasier's coals, they must be hidden away in some secret place, unknown to old Vitale, whose mind, at the thought, wandered off into wild speculation. The letter, at which he looked long and tenderly, was unquestionably in his master's character, and it expressed a solemn promise; he took the will for the deed, therefore, stubbornly maintaining that the master was a man of his word. How and where, then, had he concealed the manuscript? Upon that question he dwelt so resolutely, as almost to make his companion forget the long delay which had led to reasonable doubt. They talked on through the twilight, while the mist rose from the valley in strange, fantastic shapes that promoted a cloud of superstitious fancies, befitting time and place.

"Look yonder!" whispered the servitor; "at that hooded figure, bending low over the garden. I could swear that it is my master's. See! it retreats and comes again. What if the paper were buried there? Nay, now it is gone!"

"It is but vapor," sighed the goldsmith. "Thy master's body lies with the honored dead and may not walk again until the last hour. God rest his soul!"

"Signore, the dead are with us always. My master was a just man — a true one. If he has failed to keep his word, we shall know it from his own lips. Trust me, he will not rest in his grave."

Messer Enrico shivered, and drew his robe tighter round him. "It is cold," he murmured. "I must find my bed at the inn, and sleep. To-morrow, we will speak further of this. Consider it well, my good Vitale, and search the house again, that I may be satisfied."

"Ay, but where?" the old man asked, as they came down together. "If the thing be here, to find the hiding-place would puzzle the wise woman herself. Ah! that is not so bad a thought! I counsel the signore to make demand of her."

"The wise woman?" repeated Messer Enrico, lightly.

"Of Abano, yes, signore," answered the servant, dropping in his speech to an impres-

sive whisper; "Giralda, of the burning lake
—famous for her skill through all the country round. The secrets of the heart are revealed to her; ay, of the soul likewise! She
will unfold this, if any human being can. Go
to her, talk with her, signore."

The goldsmith smiled incredulously.
"Nay, not I!" he said. "Let her keep her
sorceries to herself. I deal not with things
of darkness."

Still old Vitale was not to be shaken in his
faith. The new idea had fastened upon him.
There lay the solution of the mystery; it was
his parting word, upon which he dwelt ear-
nestly when the garden-gate closed between
them.

Dismissing the thought of such guidance
as grotesque and irrational, Messer Enrico
returned to the inn for the repose he sorely
needed. But his night was a troubled one. In
his dreams he pursued always the same search,
which proved always unavailing, now in the
house, now in the garden, attended everywhere
by hovering phantoms of the mist that mocked
his vain endeavor.

Toward morning, he slept for a while undisturbed; till the sleep ended in a dream more disquieting than all the rest. The master stood before him, gowned and hooded as in life, but pale as death, with a look of anguish in his staring eyes; he seemed eager to speak; the white lips parted in the effort, yet no word came; at last, receding slowly, as if reluctantly drawn away by a power irresistible, the figure stretched forth its hand, beckoned, and was gone. "Stay!" the sleeper shouted; and woke, alone, at the window, whither he had dragged himself unconsciously. The moonlight gleamed upon the little square, the marble tomb beyond it; but there was no sign of life; all lay silent, motionless, deserted. Trembling with cold, he crept back to bed, where for the time his trouble ceased. "It was all a dream!" he murmured, when he woke in broad day.

For three days more he remained at Arquà, revisiting the house, urging its occupant on to investigation which brought no result. Always there was the same answer, the same suggestion of the one remedy possible in such a case. "If the signore would but consult the wise woman of Abano! The town is close at hand; and there, too, are waters, wondrous in their healing property, of which it might be well to drink a little. For, by the signore's leave, his health appears to be none of the best."

None of the best, indeed! For, though the signore, guarding his secret zealously, strove, throughout the day, with enforced cheerfulness to avert suspicion, each night the troubled dream returned. The dead master, tormented by the thought he could not speak, haunted his bedside, to renew the mute appeal and depart with hand outstretched imploringly. The dreadful presence grew more and more distressing, until the knowledge of what night would bring became an hourly torture. At the close of the third day he could bear it no longer, and, ordering his horse, prepared for flight.

But the mysterious change in him had not escaped the shrewd padrone of the inn.

"The signore will sleep at Este, then," he said; "since his health returns but slowly, and the hour is late."

"No, not at Este. I go north to Abano. They say there is virtue in its healing waters."

"Undoubtedly. The signore has been well advised."

Messer Enrico eyed the man gravely. "Tell me," he demanded; "dost thou know aught of the wise woman there, at Abano?"

"Of a surety, signore. Who does not? Her skill passes belief, and her arts are manifold. It was she who cured my brother of the fever. Had a man a devil in him, she would cast it out. Ay, more than that! All the past is known to her, and she foretells the future. She can interpret dreams."

The goldsmith started; but a look reassured him. How should the man know?

"I thank you," he said, as he rode off. "I will confide in her, if the waters fail me."

"May you be spared the need, signore, and Heaven go with you!"

So, at the first turn of the road, Messer Enrico was lost in the twilight, to be seen no more at Arquà and soon forgotten. Alighting in Abano, he found a hearty welcome, warmth, cheerfulness, and the best of provision for his comfort. Strangers, who came to drink the waters, were not infrequent there, and his arrival occasioned no remark. The mere change of scene was an encouragement. The poor, hunted victim took heart at the thought that he had returned to the land of men from the land of fearful dreams.

In this mood he composed himself to sleep, only to find all comfort spirited away. His evil destiny, defying his precautionary measures, had followed him over the hills and would not be shaken off. He slept, but the vision of the master rose before him with the old imploring look, the gesture of entreaty. Night after night, at Abano as at Arquà, the haunting terror repeated itself, and made life miserable. He could think of nothing else. And when, at last, driven half mad by the failure of simpler remedies, he sought the wise woman, it was not to demand the hiding-place of the lost manuscript, — the treasure which never had been his, — but only to be delivered from the fiend that had assumed the shape dearer to him than all others.

A mile from the town he left the level road, to follow a lonely path winding up through the woods toward a deep cleft in the hills. Around him, between the tree-trunks, volcanic rocks, seamed and scarred on their

rough sides, rose grimly, closing in the landscape. As the growth became denser, though
the sun was still high, its rays were cut off.
Upon the dim forest a strange, unearthly stillness settled down. There was no rustling of
leaves, no chirruping of birds or insects, no
movement, no sign of life other than his own.
He went on, startled by the hollow sound of
his own footsteps, fearful lest the trembling
earth should give way and engulf him suddenly; until the path, plunging lower into the
ravine, led him to a spring which bubbled
darkly over decaying leaves. He stooped to
drink. But the water, warm and brackish, en-
veloped him, as he stirred it, in a cloud of
noisome vapor. In a moment more he came
to a small lake, overhung with mist, through
which the calm surface rippled here and there
into pale, phosphorescent gleams. Dark rocks
and darker pine-trees, towering high, encircled it; its level seemed lower than the earth,
as if the dismal place lay at the very heart of
the Euganean Hills.

As the seeker stepped out upon the shore,
a shrill cry, breaking the silence, echoed from
the rocks; then reëchoed from some distant

point in answer to the call. A small boy sprang from the underbrush, and, stopping at a safe distance, began to question him.

"Your name and titles, signore. Why do you come here?"

"Enrico Capra, the goldsmith of Bergamo. They have sent me to the wise woman — Giralda, of the burning lake, if I mistake not."

"Giralda, yes, signore. This is the place. See!" Speaking, he tossed a pebble into the water. A flame flashed up for an instant, to die away in rings of fire. "It is the sign, signore. But there is no one else? The signore comes alone?"

"Quite alone."

The boy darted on into the wood; then stopped, and looking back over his shoulder, with an uncouth gesture directed the stranger to follow. Messer Enrico silently obeyed him; and in this order they proceeded along the water's edge, halfway round the lake, to a small clearing between its margin and the mountain-side. In the midst of this open space there burned what seemed a fire; but the flame leaped fitfully from the earth, leaving no ashes,

no trace of any fuel to sustain it. By the flick-
ering light a rude dwelling, hollowed out
of the cliff, could be discerned; and from its
doorway, as the two approached, a woman
stepped forward into the clearer glow, which
revealed her tall, straight figure, clad in a
flowing Eastern garment. Her face, still
young, was strong, of savage beauty. She
challenged them with a stern look in her
piercing eyes.

"Who comes with thee, Orso? What does
this man seek?"

"Peace and rest!" replied the goldsmith,
advancing toward the light. "A demon vexes
all my dreams. Release me, if this art of thine
can do so much, and I will never count the
cost. For such relief I would pay double."

"Put up the purse, signore, until the cause
is known to me. The poor skill I have avail-
eth nothing where a crime has been committed—"

"No crime, no crime! The demon comes
to me in friendly guise — as one who longs
to speak, yet cannot find the means."

The woman's face relaxed. "There, indeed, my art may be of service," she said,

gently. " Orso, to thy stone, and sleep! Follow me, signore; I must know with what I have to deal. Do not fear, speak freely."

Behind the fire, a large, smooth fragment of basaltic rock lay level with the earth. Upon its polished surface the boy, Orso, stretched himself out to sleep, as the sorceress commanded. Passing him by, she conducted Messer Enrico to her cavelike chamber in the cliff. From the low roof a lamp swung in chains; and in the narrow circle of its light stood a rough bench, beside a table with wickered flasks and wine-cups. Filling one of these, she bade the goldsmith drink. The draught of native wine composed his thoughts, and he imparted them without reserve. She listened attentively to his story, asking no questions, desiring only the master's letter, over which she pondered long. Then, urging strict silence, with her finger on her lips, she led the seeker back into the open air, where the boy still lay by the fire, sleeping now profoundly. She called to him without effect; shook him roughly, but still he did not stir. Nor did he wake when, raising him to a sitting posture, she knelt at his side, and, supporting him thus, placed the letter in his hand. His fingers closed upon the paper, he breathed heavily; then sank to rest with his head upon her shoulder.

"Orso!" she called aloud, in a tone of command. "Orso! Wake, and hear me!"

The boy stirred in his sleep, and trembled. Straining every muscle, he bent forward to stare at the stone below with fixed, wide-open eyes. She held him there in a strong, controlling grasp. And when he had ceased to struggle, she called to him again.

"Speak, Orso! What see you in the wonder-stone?"

"The square at Arquà," answered the sleeper, in a low, troubled voice. "The master's tomb is there. And there, within, the master lies asleep. No! He stirs—he wakes —he whispers to me!"

"Hark! What does he say? Listen for the words, and heed them well!"

Wondering much, Messer Enrico drew a step nearer, as if the order had been addressed to him. But the woman warned him to stand back with an angry sign.

There was a pause in which he hardly dared

to breathe. Then the boy spoke again, faintly
and more faintly.

"He would redeem his pledge. He cannot rest, even in his grave."

"Redeem it? How? Is the lost work finished, then, waiting to be found?"

"No! He shakes his head. There is nothing — nothing that may be found."

"How, then, is the master to redeem his
promise? How may one who loves him, dead
or living, bring him to eternal peace? Let
the dead command! The living will obey."

Silence, long unbroken. The very earth
seemed to stand still in breathless apprehension. There was no sound — no movement,
save from the fire at their feet. But its flame
was noiseless, like the far-off pulsation of the
attendant stars.

The answer came at last, breathed rather
than spoken, so softly that it reached Messer
Enrico's ears only in doubtful phrases which
obscured the meaning. "Enter the tomb,"
it whispered; "at night — in secret — and
take away — " What? The vital word was
lost to him in feeble mutterings; but the sorceress, bending low over the speaker, followed

them and caught their sense. As they died away, her eyes flashed triumphantly. She released the boy, laying him gently down, to unclasp his fingers and draw out the letter; then left him where he lay, asleep. And, at a sign, the bewildered goldsmith returned with her to the rock-bound chamber.

"The way is clear!" she cried; "there is but one. Didst thou not hear it?"

"All is confused," he answered, "and nothing clear to me. I heard what I cannot understand. Does the lost manuscript, by some mischance, lie buried in the tomb at Arquà?"

"No, signore; it is not that. Thy debt lies with him in the tomb, and must be cancelled. Thou art to claim the forfeit."

"The forfeit? I exacted none."

"Nay, he, himself, imposed the penalty," returned the wise woman. Speaking, she smoothed out the master's letter, and laid her finger upon a line of it. "Look! This written word still binds him. His restless spirit craves release. Cancel the bond and set him free!"

With a look of horror Messer Enrico started back.

"Never, to save my soul!" he cried. "I never can do that."

"The peace of the master is at stake, as well as thine," she said, calmly. "His prayer brings absolution. Dismiss the childish fear, and do his bidding."

"The fiend's prayer, not the master's! Heeding it, how may I find peace on earth? The world will hold me guilty of a mortal sin."

"The dead master commits his secret to our keeping," replied the sorceress; "it is ours to hold and guard through all eternity. The world will never know."

Messer Enrico sank, shuddering, upon his knees, and hid his face. "If I could believe!" he moaned.

Moving to his side, the wise woman stooped over him compassionately; there were tears in her eyes as she touched his shoulder with a gentle pressure.

"How to persuade one that will not be persuaded?" she murmured. "I do but waste my words. Go back, signore, to Abano. The evil dream will come again to prove that I speak honestly. And when all doubt is over, command my service and the boy's, to aid thee in thy act of faith; it must be done secretly, and with despatch. A word will summon us to Arquà."

"Heaven save me from it!" cried the goldsmith, recovering his self - command, "and grant that we may meet no more! The worth of thy infernal counsels — name the price! I would go free of thee forever."

"Nay, not yet!" was the quiet answer. "I would be justified. Wait for the fitting hour — the proof which time will surely bring. Wait, signore, wait until we meet at Arquà."

He had raised his hand to fling the purse at her feet. But her gentleness disarmed him. He put away the money and, turning silently from the place, went down to Abano in the dusk, he knew not how. There, among men, the spell under which he labored was broken. All that had lately passed became at once unreal. Laughing at fear, he went to bed, to sleep. But he had dismissed the fear too lightly. The spectre was not laid. More dreadful than before, it now bent over him reproachfully; now touched him with an icy hand. The deadly chill remained, when he woke, shrieking. So, in the space of one short night, was the wise woman justified. Here was the proof she had foretold, which time must surely bring.

III

DAYBREAK at Arquà! Though all the low-land lay hidden in its veil of mist, the sky's unclouded arch assured a fine, bright morning. Old Vitale, bestirring himself, flung open the shutters of the master's house, and welcomed the sunshine with a glow of satis-faction. The day was here, at last, when, by appointment, the noble Lord of Padua, Francesco di Carrara, would come again to fulfil the conditions of his trust. To-day the master's library would be transferred to the patron's keeping; the closed cabinets would be unlocked, the rare volumes, so carefully protected, one by one would be removed. All was in perfect order, with every seal un-broken. For the hundredth time, the faith-ful watch-dog convinced himself of this. In a few hours his new master must arrive to

take possession ; perhaps, even now, the short
journey was more than half accomplished ;
there might be signs of his approach upon the
Paduan road, which the upper western window commanded for a mile or more. To
that outlook the old man climbed in nervous expectation. The clustered houses of the
town were just below him, and beyond them
shone the narrow ribbon of the highway,
white and still, without a speck upon it. But,
while he looked, the quiet town itself woke
from calmness to commotion. He heard the
sound of hurrying feet, and saw the little
square before the church rapidly fill up with
a curious crowd, drawn together by some
rumor of a startling nature. All eyes were
fixed upon the master's tomb with looks of
mingled wonder and dismay. Old Vitale
rushed down among the curious faces, to
make, in his turn, an incredible discovery.
The tomb had been forced open in the
night; one broken slab of marble lay on the
ground where it had fallen. Yet the town
had slept quietly, without the slightest hint
of such disturbance. What ruffian could have
wrought, secretly and silently, this act of in-

famous irreverence? For what unholy purpose was the sacred dust within thus vio-
lated? These were questions that each one
asked, that none dared answer. All dreaded
to pursue them further, to define the extent
of the theft, to lay bare the effect that should
explain the cause.

The wonder grew when the task of investigation was undertaken by the parish priest,
and the opening in the tomb proved too small
to admit him. The theft, if theft it was, must,
then, have been committed either by a child
or by a dwarf. Under the priest's guidance a
boy of the inn, solemnly charged to speak the
truth, crawled into the sarcophagus, and furnished evidence to be publicly announced with
due formality. The master's face was still se-
rene, undisturbed and undisfigured. His only
ornaments — the jewelled clasp of his robe
and the ring upon his left hand — remained
intact. But the right hand, that master hand
to which the world acknowledged an ines-
timable debt, was wanting. It had been cut
off adroitly at the wrist, and secreted or carried away. A thorough search revealed no
trace of it. For this mutilation alone had the

impious offender performed his deed of darkness. Thus were the cause and effect of his unaccountable desecration explained and verified.

Following hard upon this announcement, the Lord of Padua rode into the square with all his retinue. Immediately every door was closed and every house ransacked at his command. He proclaimed the theft a capital offence, promising rewards and honors to any, high or low, whose testimony should convict the criminal; all without avail. A week passed, and neither the severed hand nor any clue to the place of its concealment came to light. Then he restored the tomb, consecrating it anew with fitting rites and ceremonies, leaving the mystery of the crime and its solution to after ages; still without avail. Centuries have elapsed; the threats and promises bequeathed to the world by Francesco di Carrara are all forgotten. He, himself, is remembered only as the false patron, who, dispersing the master's library, betrayed his sacred trust. But the marble monument remains at Arquà, an object of veneration. And today the humble villager, deciphering its worn

inscription, pauses to repeat one line significantly, and to dispute it. "*Hic tegit ossa Petrarce!* Nay, not so!" he insists. "For the
right hand is wanting." Ask him the why
and wherefore, and he shakes his head. He
has inherited the mystery, but not the means
to answer you.

The ancient church of Santa Maria Mag-
giore, at Bergamo, is the city's pride and glory.
Great artists have enriched it; priest and patron and valiant captain sleep within its walls,
under vast canopies of sculptured marble. The
pavement - stones protect the humbler dead;
but many a name, once graven there, is gone
forever, obliterated by the feet of passing generations. And among these lies Messer Enrico Capra, the famous goldsmith, thus effaced
from memory, lost until the judgment-day.
In that obscure grave, unknown, unimagined,
is a wondrous treasure, richer than any that
the church displays. The disciple survived
his master by more than half a decade. On
his death - bed, to the devoted serving - man,
Marcello, he gave his last instructions: These
were to enter the closed chamber in his house,

to take therefrom a certain golden casket and place it in his coffin; to do this alone, secretly; and, on his life, to let none know. When the hour came, the man discharged the letter of his duty, if not the spirit. For, amazed at the beauty of the goldsmith's masterpiece, he began to speculate upon its purpose, to wonder why this marvel had been wrought, what it was designed to hold; till, yielding to his curiosity, he forced the lock, and was startled to find within only what seemed a human hand. He mistook this for some saintly relic; but while he looked, it crumbled, lost its shape, and fell into a heap of ashes. Then, with averted eyes, fearing to look upon his master's face, he hid the precious casket and its contents under the dead man's robe, and closed the coffin-lid. None knew, none suspected; all knowledge of the wonder died with him; this world will never share it. The treasures of a nameless grave are guarded well.

WINTER ISLAND

WINTER ISLAND

I

IT was half-past nine o'clock, and Dr.
Holderness had so nearly finished his
packing, that he decided to leave what remained until morning, and to smoke one or
two pipes by way of refreshment before bedtime. He sat down at the open window, and,
tilting back his chair luxuriously, listened to
the crickets' call which intensified the stillness of the September night. How exceptional this place was in its repose! His first
look at the dismantled room had been one
of satisfaction; but now there stole into his
mind that peculiar sadness which closes all
life's little enterprises, whether they be
wholly agreeable, or otherwise, — a sadness
born of the flight of Time and the thought
that the term of experience has made us so
much older. This man's term of six weeks
in the wilderness had been an experiment
which, upon the whole, had succeeded

wonderfully well. Rest had been its main
object; for Holderness was on the surgical
staff of a great city hospital, and after his ex-
hausting July service had joined a comrade
in arms who suggested a complete change
for them both. They had chosen Winter
Island, because it lies twenty miles from the
nearest railroad, on the very margin of the
wide tract of forest, lake, and mountain that
stretches over New England's northern bound-
ary into Canada. The peaceful little Maine
village, in a hollow among the hills, almost
encircled by a rushing tributary of the Andros-
coggin, has justified its name literally, perhaps,
in more than one late winter freshet; and,
at all seasons, its insulation from the world's
disturbing influences is well - nigh perfect.
Holderness, by chance, had found a rare
opportunity to test its advantages in this respect. His companion, Dr. Hardy, had been
summoned back to town prematurely; and
for more than a fortnight the young surgeon
had lived on alone in tranquil isolation, —
doubtfully, at first, then gratefully, after his
resolve to employ this leisure in writing up
a certain difficult operation which he had

lately performed with improved instruments
of his own contrivance. The result had confirmed his belief in their practical value, and
a long descriptive article upon the process
was already shaping itself in his mind. There
could be no better moment for working it
out than this one, left free to him unexpectedly. He would begin the important paper,
at least, and finish it, or not, as time served.

The days had flown, the time - limit was
reached; in another twenty - four hours the
city's turmoil and the round of professional
cares would overwhelm him. The revised
manuscript lay packed away in the bottom of
his trunk; he could never have accomplished
all that so swiftly in town. He was ready to
go back, fired by the cheerful glow which
completion of a long task always brings; yet
there was enchantment in these perfect days
and nights whereof the only sounds were
Nature's; they had cast their spell upon him,
and he would surely miss the charm of it,
cockney at heart though he knew himself
to be.

The window opened upon an old-fashioned
garden, stretching in a succession of terraces

toward the river-bank where a fringe of pop-
lars defined itself vaguely against the mellow
stars. As he looked up at the dark tree-tops,
remembering that there was a waning moon
soon to rise beyond them, the cry of the
crickets suddenly ceased, and, through the
stillness thus made oppressive, he fancied that
he heard a faint sound upon the garden-path.
Was it a step, or the rustle of a garment? In
either case, it must come from one of the
women; for, certainly, the master of the
house, John Winter, could not bear the bur-
den of his two hundred pounds so lightly as
that. After a breathless moment bringing
no definite conclusion, Holderness rose and
looked out. All lay hushed in a shroud of
darkness, deepened by the restless glories of
the sky through which a splendid meteor
trailed its long ellipse. The crickets chirped
again, louder than before. No one stirred in
the garden; its freshness exhilarated him; he
would stroll down to the river and watch the
moon come up behind the smooth crest of
Bald Pate Mountain, — for the last time.

Refilling his pipe, accordingly, Holderness
followed the main path between clumps of

late-blossoming flowers,—mignonette, pinks,
and verbenas, making the night air fragrant,
— until it had brought him to the edge of the
second terrace. Here he turned into a side
path bordered with a row of currant-bushes
which formed a dividing line between the
flowers and the kitchen-garden, lying below.
At the farther end of the walk stood a wooden
bench, and from that point a gap in the shrub-
bery gave a glimpse of the distant mountain
range; already above its wooded peaks the stars
were dim in the glow of the rising moon.
Holderness knew the spot well; he had often
sat there, undisturbed, through half the night.
But now, as he threw himself down with a
grateful sense of solitude, his ears caught a
strange sound, and immediately he became
conscious that he was not alone. He listened.
Yes, there could be no doubt; it was the
sound of sobbing. Some one, close by, — a
woman, of course, — had given way to pas-
sionate grief. He moved to the brink of the
terrace, pushing the leaves aside gently, and
looked down. A few feet away, on the bank
below, a young girl had flung herself face
downward in the long grass, and was crying

as though her heart would break. Even in the dark Holderness must have recognized that slender figure; and, while he looked, the moon rose over the valley, flooding the whole place with light. He could see distinctly the heavy coil of brown hair, the thin neck and thinner arms, bare to the elbow, protruding from a quaint, ill-fitting dress of a fashion all its own, — and these things were unmistakable. It was only Barbara Winter, the daughter of this quiet house. He had overtaken her, that very afternoon, on her way home from the district school where she taught the younger children; she had spoken then and later, at the table, with all her usual cheerfulness. What misfortune could have overcome her since? Some childish cloud of the moment, probably, that would pass away before morning; and yet, for the moment, he was eager to know.

In spite of this whim, however, Holderness hesitated to intrude upon a sorrow so acute as this seemed to be. And, while he waited in doubt, a distant voice called the girl by name. She stirred, but he drew back in time to avoid discovery.

The voice came nearer, sharply raised in a tone that he knew to be her mother's: —

"Barbara — Barbara! Where are you?" it cried.

Then there were steps, and the girl, finding no escape, answered faintly. The steps approached, while with an exclamation of surprise the questioning voice continued: —

"Why, Barbara, what ails you, child? What is it? Tell me."

The only audible reply was a burst of tears, but, from the movement accompanying it, Holderness knew that the girl had flung herself into her mother's arms. He had an irritating desire to hear the explanation of this trouble, but would not yield to it. The confidence that must follow could be no affair of his. He had no right to listen a moment longer; he withdrew noiselessly, therefore, and returned to the house, priding himself unduly upon his own discretion. With the temptation removed, his idle curiosity melted away. Upon reaching his room, he saw at the first glance a pile of books thrown down near one of the locked trunks into which he had meant to pack them. Among these was

a volume of essays by a new writer, — the subject of much discussion, as he remembered,
in the great world to which he was returning. They called it there the book of the
year; but, cross-questioned upon it the day
before he left, he had been forced into a confession of ignorance. Here it lay, staring him
in the face, with its leaves still uncut. The
night was absurdly young for sleep. He would
begin this great work now. He filled his pipe
again, cut the first pages mechanically, skim-
ming them as he did so; then turned back to
read them slowly and thoughtfully; and was
soon absorbed in the reading.

II

JOHN WINTER, the American Giant, as he
had been playfully called in college days, of
the heroic type, still strong as an ox at forty-
five, was a complete failure in the eyes of his
relatives and of those friends that were left
to him. Understanding perfectly their judgment upon his case, he not only acknowledged its justice, but accepted it as final. He
had been caught in an eddy of life's current,

and, reconciled to his place there, made no effort to regain the course of the stream. His father and grandfather were famous men of their time; the oracle of early association, if interrogated, must have promised him a brilliant future. But the flock was large, and he soon turned into its one black sheep. His college life proved, from the first, as wild and idle as he could make it; until in the sophomore year he was charged with uproarious misdemeanor, and sentenced to a year's suspension. Transferred for this season of study and repentance to the abandoned family farm at Winter Island, he became the idol of the whole township, repaying its admiration by turning over a new and most disconcerting leaf in his Liber Amoris with a reckless offer of marriage to the village beauty. The girl's character was good; she was estimable in her way; but her way was far from being that of John Winter's family, whose strong disapproval and strenuous interference only made matters worse, however, hastening the end. When the time arrived for his return to college, John Winter had come of age and into a modest inheritance,—and was a married man.

The family endeavored, at first, to make the best of a bad business. There had been no open quarrel, and there should be none. John's wife was received with a show of cordiality which grew more and more perfunctory. She was a country girl of moderate ability and intelligence, unrefined, uncultivated. She could not understand the family aims and pursuits; but she fully understood its disappointment in the marriage, as well as the false position into which she was thrust by so-called intercourse with her husband's circle of friends. Finding the ordeal insufferable, she shrank from it more and more, until her husband, in his visits to town, was left to deal with it alone. As his family increased, these visits became infrequent; the old fire died down in him, and was replaced by a lazy indifference to all that went on beyond the narrow limits of Winter Island. Nominally the centre of that small system, he was in fact subordinate to his wife, whose quiet influence, all for good, developed new tastes, and made him the most domestic of mankind. She had a fondness for reading, due to a sense of neglect in early life which she desired to counter-

act. She encouraged him to buy books that
he might read them aloud in the long winter
evenings, and the acquisition of a library grew
to be his pet extravagance, which he cherished in spite of sharp cuts at his income
dealt him by his unlucky star. The books
brought consolation when these money losses
were followed by the death of two children,
and served their turn again when his one remaining child, Barbara, showed signs of interest in them. The transformation of the
idle reprobate, John Winter, into a pious
instructor of youth was almost miraculous.
Could his own instructors have witnessed it,
they would certainly have doubted the evidence of their senses.

He had passed middle age, and had taken
his first step upon life's long, level table-
land. Old age may begin at forty-five, as New
England's genial Autocrat of medicine and
philosophy declares it does; but, in the beginning, outward demonstration of the solemn
truth is mercifully spared us. The path has
not yet entered upon its decline. We have
ceased to climb, that is all. At this point in
his career, John Winter grew optimistic. He

had suffered displacement and, with it, the
loss of his golden opportunities; he was a
poor man, hopelessly removed from all that
made life dear to his former boon companions, who looked askance at him when they
looked at all; yet, as the country people said,
it was better to be " at the head of the poor
than at the tail of the rich," especially when
one possessed the compensations of a devoted
wife and child, happy in their lot, with no
vain longings for a world unknown to them.
Why should he give it another thought?
Having them and a roof, such as it was, to
shelter them, he had assuredly more than he
deserved.

It was under this roof which contentment
and its twin virtue of resignation thus controlled that Robert Holderness and his friend
had so long been quartered. Their coming
seemed a windfall to the family; Mrs. Winter
labored for their comfort, and found them far
from exacting. Indeed, on the day of their
arrival, Hardy, eyeing a book on the hall
table, whispered that to have a host who read
Balzac was worth, in itself, the price they
paid. John Winter perplexed them much

until they had picked up here and there the fragments of his story. No allusion to a former state ever came from him, however. He was always inclined to be reticent, and these young men had too much of the city in them to please him thoroughly. But he gave them at once the freedom of his library, expanding, by degrees, into a kind of un-demonstrative geniality of which, at first, they supposed him incapable. After Hardy's de-parture, Holderness saw a little more of the philosophic landlord, and they became, in consequence, better friends. On this last day, Winter had even expressed a hope of seeing the surgeon there again, another year; then, as if to show that the hope was not wholly based upon his pocket, he had volunteered to drive Holderness down to the station on the morrow. His horses needed exercise, he said; the forty miles, there and back, would do them good; and Holderness had accepted the invi-tation in the friendly spirit that prompted it.

Now, after half an hour's reading, Hol-derness tossed his book aside, and looked at his watch. It was not so very late, even for Arcadia; John Winter might possibly be found sitting up with his philosophy; he would go into the library for a night-cap and a quiet word. As he prepared for this, he heard once more a step outside his window, — this time, there could be no question of it; then, while he turned that way, a hand tapped gently at the pane.

"Who is it?" he asked, advancing toward the window, and to his surprise finding Mrs. Winter there.

"May I come?" she whispered; but before he could reply, she had stepped into the room with a hurried word of explanation. "I want to tell you something, — it won't take long."

She was a year or two older than her husband, and the beauty which captivated him had faded from her face. Its sharpened features had settled into rigid lines seldom relaxed by a smile. Holderness would have described her as a typical New England woman of the severer sort, dry, unemotional, hard even. Now, all this was changed; her sallow cheeks were flushed; there were tears in her eyes; she seemed unnerved and strongly agitated. His mind instantly connected the change with what had taken place in the

garden, while he had been an involuntary
witness; but he was careful to betray no knowledge of it.

Bringing a chair, he begged her to sit
down. "What is it?" he inquired. "Tell
me! How can I help you?"

"I don't know," she sighed, as she dropped
into the seat; "Barbara —"

He was right, then; but, still on his guard,
he only continued the inquiries sympathetically: "Is Barbara ill? Is anything wrong?"

"Not ill," the woman answered, "but
something's wrong. I don't know as it's
right to tell you, — perhaps not. But I've
decided to, anyway; so, there it is!"

He waited for her to go on, though she
had come to a full stop helplessly, picking
at a fold of her dress with nervous fingers.
Mystified now, and a thousand miles from the
truth, he broke at last the constrained silence.

"Well! what do you mean? I don't understand at all."

She looked him full in the face, and the
truth flashed through his mind, before she
spoke it.

"No, you don't understand," she said, in a

peculiar tone from which all emotion had died away into an impersonal statement of the fact; "I did n't either, until I made her tell me. I found her just crying her eyes out of her head, because you are going away. She can't bear it, she says; she loves you, that 's all."

"Barbara ?" stammered Holderness. "She is a mere child, — there must be some mistake. She cannot have asked you to tell me this."

"No," returned Mrs. Winter, with the same intent look which disturbed him, though he did not yet avert his own; "no, she don't dream of it. She would hate me for telling you. But the mischief's done. She is seventeen, and knows her own mind, I guess, or thinks she does. I have told you, because — because it couldn't make matters worse for her than they are."

Holderness turned uneasily, and looked out of the window with sightless eyes. Had the acres of distant forest burst suddenly into flame, he would hardly have known it.

"I am very sorry," said he; "I had no idea of this. It will pass away and be forgotten, when I am gone."

Mrs. Winter had already risen, colorless now, but in perfect self-possession. "That's about the best we can look for, I suppose," she said, dryly.

"I can only say again that I am extremely sorry. I cannot account for this. There has been no fault of mine, you may be sure."

"Fault, no! I didn't expect there was." Going, she turned back at the window. "Mr. Winter means to drive you down to-morrow, don't he?"

"Yes."

"You'd better not say anything to him, then. It wouldn't be quite fair to Barbara, if it got round."

"Certainly not —" Holderness began; but she was already gone.

As if her return were a danger to be feared, he immediately closed the window and bolted it; then, after locking his door, he paced the room for a long time. This news was most annoying and unpleasant. What evil spirit had incited Mrs. Winter to her confidence? Why could not she have held her tongue, and let him go in peace? Of course, she had been moved by impulse, with a kind of forlorn hope that love might create love, turning her child's despair to exultation. That had been as clear to him as if frankly admitted. But love did not work in that way. Even she, herself, the moment her senses returned, had perceived how baseless the hope was, and had immediately abandoned it, accepting all that his surprise and dismay expressed, without the need of explicit verbal confirmation. For this intuitive good judgment on her part he was profoundly grateful. But Barbara! It was too bad! That awkward country girl, untrained, unformed, so young for her years that he had associated them with childhood! Was he to blame, then? No, certainly not; he had talked with her, to be sure, but never in terms even remotely suggestive of tenderness. Well, nothing more could be said or done. By this time to-morrow he would be safely out of the poor child's range. Her dream was over; and she would get over it, as he had declared. But it was absurd, preposterous! And with these words, oft-repeated, Holderness busied himself with his trunks; then went to bed, and, finally, to sleep, still dwelling on the absurdity of his adventure.

He woke late, and though the unfortunate affair was uppermost in his mind, he had little time to consider it. At breakfast, Mrs. Winter's manner was as simple and natural as he could have desired; but he did not care to be alone with her, so that when her husband left the table hurriedly to bring round the horses, Holderness got up with him. As Barbara had not appeared, he accounted for the absence in his own way, already congratulating himself upon an escape without seeing her. He waited on the steps while his trunks were stowed away in the wagon; John Winter climbed to his seat with the reins; Mrs. Winter presented herself at the door, to bid him good-bye, offering her hand; as he took it, there came a step, and Barbara stood before him. He had a painful consciousness that she was dressed to do him honor, in all the finery which she possessed; and, for the moment, he was disconcerted even more by this than by her sudden entrance upon the scene. Meanwhile, she wished him a pleasant journey in the lightest of tones. Then he recovered himself completely, as he fancied, and they shook hands without obvious embarrassment. He

took his place at her father's side. While the
wagon whirled away, he looked back to wave
a final farewell. They stood at the door, and
he was gone. But with the dust from his departing wheels still in the air, the child turned
upon the woman, and cried in a broken
voice:—

"*Mother!* He knows, — I am sure of it.
MOTHER! *You have told him!*"

III

IT was not altogether his gentle regard for
Barbara's welfare which, during the next few
years, prevented Dr. Holderness from adopt-
ing her father's friendly suggestion of a second
visit to Winter Island ; though that influence
would undoubtedly have served to keep him
away in the following summer, had even the
bare possibility of such a plan occurred to him.
The correspondence of dates brought her foolish little romance up very vividly ; but he
was at Heidelberg then, and saw his waning
moon over the castle ruins. After that, her
story became unimportant, to be dismissed
with a smile when chance revived it. His

own interests multiplied; he grew in experience and reputation, and had adventures far more exciting than that pale passion which seemed as though it were left over from the last century. Then, more than two years later came the adventure which he had believed to be impossible, — the sad experience thus far lacking in his complex life. At an unguarded moment he fell desperately in love with the most fascinating and least scrupulous of her sex, — a reigning belle and arch-coquette, to whom all men but the right one were so much food for powder. Though the young surgeon had distinction enough to make him an interesting conquest, his refusal was a mere question of time. The time came; the blow stunned Holderness, at first; but he rallied from it, and was actually on the point of tempting fate with her again, when she threw down her arms to accept the millionaire, twice her age, who had long been the secret goal of her ambition. No one ever knew the sharpness of the trial to her latest victim. He kept his own counsel so skilfully that his closest friends could but surmise the truth; and that cynical devotion to a life of celibacy, which followed, was indicated, rather than expressed, by his attitude toward the love-passages in other lives. Holderness, master of his profession, could look at a mortal wound without flinching, — even though the wound were his own.

Precisely five years had passed since that forgotten summer in the wilderness, when the surgeon, close upon middle age and now regarded as a confirmed bachelor, once more turned his face to the north; not toward Winter Island, which had no place in his thoughts, but toward a point, miles away from that village, in the forest's very heart, where certain friends were encamped upon one of the Rangeley Lakes. Holderness had been for several hours in the train, and, as it approached his destination, becoming tired of his books and papers, he tossed them all away, to consider the flying landscape. Soon he perceived in its more prominent features a familiar look, reminding him of the fact which, until then, he had dismissed as insignificant: the fact, namely, that in this new journey he was really retracing his old course. Then, while the past drifted back into his mind, he grew interested in the present prospect, and fancied that he recognized even the fields and the farmhouses. He spread out the rude railway map of his time-table to study the names upon it, suddenly remembering that the station where he must leave the train was also a point of approach to Winter Island. There were two or three ways of reaching the outlying village, as he knew; this was not the one he had formerly chosen, he was sure; but, surely, this station must be the very place to which John Winter had driven him on the final day. He wondered that he had not thought of it before; he wondered also if his drive to the camp would be over that same road, straight through the scene of the odd little episode in his career which, lying dormant in his memory for years, was now awakened. The wonder would soon solve itself; for they were due in five minutes at the place, — a junction of local importance, where, as he remembered, a busy town had sprung up. He made his preparations to alight, and waited. The train flew on; then, at the sound of a whistle, the brakes were put down, and it stopped sharply.

Opening his window, he looked forward along the line. They were close upon the junction; he could see its roofs and spires; but the way was blocked by another train which had come to a standstill, and its passengers swarmed out upon the embankment. Holderness, scenting an accident in which a surgeon might be of service, was soon among them. What had happened? he asked; and learned that a fireman on the advance train, leaning out of the cab-window, had come into collision with a telegraph-pole, and was seriously hurt. This was the spot where he had fallen, but he had been carried into the baggage-car, around the open doors of which stood the inevitable, curious crowd in futile discussion of the mishap. Holderness hurried on, noting dark stains in the gravel which showed that the injured man had bled profusely, and overhearing whispered comment that he could not understand.

"She's one of the right sort!" said one.

"Yes," was the answer; "that's a woman worth having."

"Let me pass, please," said Holderness, quietly. "I am a surgeon."

The crowd parted at once, and he sprang lightly into the car. The fireman, white and senseless, lay upon the floor, his head resting in the lap of a young girl who stanched the wound with a compress of handkerchiefs, while the conductor and other officials stared at her in helpless approbation. As Holderness knelt at her side, she looked up, and in spite of time's changes, which in her case had been altogether for the better, he immediately recognized Barbara Winter. The flush overspreading her pale face showed that he was not forgotten, but she only whispered:—

"I tried to help. Nobody seemed to know what to do."

"Quite right!" he whispered back. "Don't move,—let me look at him!"

The flow of blood had ceased, but the examination disclosed to his practised eye and hand a fracture of the skull. As he silently replaced the bandage, the conductor asked him if the man was dead.

"No," he said; "thanks to this young lady, who has made it possible to save him. Go on at once,—very slowly." Then, turning to the girl : "Can you stay just as you are, a few moments longer ? " he inquired.

"Of course !" she replied.

While the train glided up to the platform, Holderness ascertained that the fireman's home was in the town they were approaching. By his orders the man, still unconscious, was carried into an inner room of the station to await the improvised ambulance, and a messenger was despatched to inform his wife. Barbara, meanwhile, had disappeared, probably joining her father, who stood in the crowd through which they hurried. Holderness remained in charge, performing the operation with the assistance of the local surgeon. All this took time; two hours had elapsed and it was nearly three in the afternoon, when, leaving his patient comfortable and likely to recover, he turned from the sick - room for consideration of his own affairs. At the door he encountered John Winter, who had been unwilling to drive away without greeting his old friend. How did Holderness happen to be here, and what was his objective point ? Oh, yes; he knew Great Bear Camp perfectly ; the only way to it, as

Holderness had guessed, went straight through Winter Island; but the road beyond the village into the depth of the forest was very rough, — it was too late to reach the camp that night; so much the better, for, of course, his friend would pass the night with him. About this there could be no kind of question, and none was permitted. The horse stood at the door; Holderness must be hungry as well as tired; they would drive first to the hotel, or, better still, to the restaurant at the station, where Barbara waited for them, where he could eat, drink, and smoke in peace before going on.

So, in the friendliest spirit, John Winter caught up the reins, leaving Holderness no excuse for resistance which would not seem to the last degree ungracious. An hour later, sharing with Barbara the back seat of the wagon, he flung to the winds all doubts that oppressed him when his course was shaped so swiftly in the one way he could not have foreseen. The momentary embarrassment had worn itself out, inasmuch as his companion gave not the smallest sign of a similar feeling. That this could be the Barbara Winter he

once knew was extremely difficult to realize.
The awkward child, whose inconvenient admiration he had eluded, seemed to have developed mentally as well as physically ; and
in her place sat a full-grown woman of exceptional beauty, somewhat reserved, it is
true, yet entirely at ease. Much impressed
by the change, he suffered no detail of it to
escape him ; he noticed the delicacy of her
complexion, the fineness of her hair, the
clear light in her deep blue eyes. Her manners were sympathetic and refined. If her
dress failed to follow the latest fashion, it
was all in good taste. She had grace, gentleness, charm, — the charm of an unconven-
tional simplicity which attracted him more
and more. Her admiration was no longer a
disturbing element; on the contrary, he found
a glow of pleasure in the thought that this
girl cared for him, and had even gone so far
as to confess it. There was nothing to show
that she knew of the indiscretion which had
betrayed her secret. He became convinced
that she did not know, and the conviction
placed him upon a kind of vantage - ground
which added piquancy to his sudden interest

in this marvelous changeling. He expressed
admiration for her now, complimenting the
presence of mind she had displayed at the
time of the accident. She had, undoubtedly,
saved the man's life. Where had she acquired
her skill? How had she known what to do?
She blushed, and could not answer. But her
father, overhearing, explained that Barbara
had a clear head, not easily lost. Then she
immediately changed the subject, and Holderness found her more charming than ever.

As they drew near the house, he began
to wonder how Mrs. Winter would receive
him. His sudden arrival must recall to her
their painful interview on the eve of his
departure, — so unpleasantly, perhaps, as to
make him an unwelcome guest even for a
single night. In her surprise she might go
so far as to manifest her dissatisfaction. That
possibility was anything but agreeable; why
had he not awakened to it earlier, and pre-
cluded it by some hastily framed excuse for
declining her husband's urgent hospitality?
That would have given John Winter mortal
offence, it is true; he hoped the wife would
understand this, and forgive him for impal-

ing himself upon the other horn of the dilemma. He was immensely relieved to find
that she showed no feeling but one of cordiality; the fact being, as Holderness did
not know, that she had been prepared for
his visit by a message from one of the vil-
lagers whom John Winter had seen at the
station. His word, brought early in the afternoon, thus smoothed the way. The guest,
warmly greeted, was installed in his old
room where nothing had changed. Only the
face he saw in the glass looked five years
older, — that was all. The evening meal was
served with its former profusion; his hostess
had remembered certain dishes which he
liked, and pleasantly drew his attention to
them. Like Barbara she had gained in
ease. As they sat around the fire afterward,
the talk never languished into awkward
pauses; but it remained for the most part
impersonal, until the women took their
leave with many good wishes for his comfort. Then the host produced whiskey over
which they lingered to a late hour in the
old friendly way. John Winter, on pain of
displeasure, demanded a longer visit from

him on his return from the camp. And Holderness, with a smile, pledged himself to provide for this. He went to bed feeling that the dreaded ordeal had taken so happy a turn as practically to prove no ordeal at all.

His hurried departure the next morning left opportunity for little more than an exchange of commonplaces. Barbara did not come down, and her mother explained that she suffered from a severe headache; the accident of yesterday having been somewhat of a shock to the child's nerves, of which she now felt the effect. As if to assure him that this explanation was the true one, Mrs. Winter, herself, did far more than mere civility required in seconding urgently her husband's wish for their guest's return. She exacted a solemn promise that he would not fail them. In considering afterward her demeanor toward him, Holderness found himself perplexed and even a little annoyed by it. Some slight indication that a wholesome fear of him existed in her mind would have been more flattering in the circumstances. Did such a fear really exist beneath the cleverly assumed disguise of her welcome

and farewell? Was Mrs. Winter turning
into a woman of the world with perfunctory
phrases of courtesy ever at command? Or
had the old forlorn hope in a love-match
returned with such force as to make this
courting of his presence entirely genuine?
She, herself, had married for love a man
brought up in cities; she was happy, and
longed to see her daughter's happiness assured in the same way. This might be her
simple-hearted motive,—the more probable
one of the two, perhaps. But Holderness,
after long study over the problem, gave it
up in despair. He decided, however, to limit
the return visit to a single day, which could
do no harm and need give no offence, if he
worded his excuses properly. Professional
engagements which could neither be postponed nor disproved should call him imper-
atively back to town. Yet this resolution
was no sooner taken than he found it cautious
to absurdity. If one day, why not three? if
three, why not a week? a week, after all, was
so short a time!

IV

From the moment when Holderness lightly reproached himself for over-caution in this case of delicacy he was, without perceiving it in the least, a lost man. We are never so easily deluded as by our own selves in ascribing acts that spring from complex motives to some very simple one, chosen for its plausibility to serve as advocate at the bar of judgment. But the atmosphere of Great Bear Camp was well adapted to clear away his mental cobwebs. The little band of sportsmen and guides assembled there numbered ten in all, and of these his old friend, Hardy, was the controlling spirit. The evenings around the fire were merry; the cold, still nights induced refreshing sleep; by day, the deer could be stalked with sufficient success to make the sport exciting. Yet in the vast solitudes of lake and forest Holderness, left alone with his taciturn guide, found ample time to consider pursuits beyond that of game. With a definite past to look back upon and a shadowy future lying in ambush, the wilderness began to suggest something more than mere present enjoyment. It was a breathing-place, a turning-point in the great labyrinth of life, giving him a glimpse of many roads.

So, in one of these reflective moods, it occurred to Holderness that there might be some special reason for finding a week at Winter Island short indeed. The new presence of Barbara Winter haunted him more and more, until he had contrasted it favorably with that of every other woman known to him, — especially, with the one who had played him false. That love of a misguided past seemed downright madness now. The simple beauty and gentle ways of this country girl held no such intoxication in them ; he could contemplate them calmly; but he did so with increased respect which passed into a deeper feeling. He woke one morning to find that he loved her for her strength of character, her unaffected modesty, — for the qualities that he distinguished and those that he divined. Here was his hope of happiness, so long relinquished, presented in a new and lovelier form, awaiting but a word to claim it, since she had already confessed her love

for him. As he recalled the circumstances
of that confession, in his changed attitude of
mind he pronounced himself blind and a fool
for not appreciating its true value upon the
instant. Viewing her always now in a glori-
fied light, he forgot the transformation time
had worked in them both, and failed to understand his former state of apathy. Happily,
as he believed, it was not too late to repair
this fault. But that could not be done in a
single day. Even the week now set apart for
reparation seemed painfully short. Upon some
pretext or another the return visit must be
prolonged, — indefinitely.

Fortune was the kind host with whom
Holderness had not reckoned. He fixed his
day for leaving the camp, and found means
to give John Winter due notice thereof, —
avoiding, however, any positive statement as
to the length of his stay. Then, on the very
eve of this journey, he stumbled in the dark
over a twisted root within a few feet of the
camp - fire, fell heavily, made an agonizing
effort to get up, and, a moment later, was
brought in with a broken leg. Dr. Hardy
promptly took charge of the case which

proved to be a simple fracture of the tibia,
not at all alarming; in a month or two he
would walk again as well, if not better than
ever, — it was rather a good thing than otherwise. Holderness smiled at the professional
jest which covered an unsuspected grain of
truth. There was no need of trumping up a
shallow pretext now. To remain at Winter
Island indefinitely would be the most natural thing in the world, — a thing hardly to
be evaded, in fact. Sustained by this cheerful
prospect through the long, restless night, he
accepted his fate without a murmur; and
morning found him in such high spirits that
his friends marvelled at his plucky way of
taking the annoying accident, more distressing to them, apparently, than to the actual
victim. They naturally attributed this lightness of heart to the long surgical experience
which enabled him to regard all accident as
matter for summary treatment, without the
shedding of useless tears, even when it struck
home. Naturally, likewise, Holderness did
not attempt to undeceive them.

Hardy had patched up the injured leg with
a temporary dressing, and under his direction

the guides set to work at once upon a litter
of maple - boughs. When Holderness was
established therein at an early hour of the
morning, which luckily proved fine, with his
leg protected by pillows from any possible
strain, he declared that he had never been
more comfortable in his life. He bore the
journey and all that followed it without
flinching. When night came, and the bone
was secured in place by a plaster bandage, he
lay in his comfortable bed at Winter Island,
all ready, he said, for convalescence. As he
had foreseen, John Winter and his wife set
no limit to their measure of sympathetic hospitality; they would not permit him to think
of the long homeward journey, before he was
able to walk; and they agreed with Dr. Hardy
in accounting the misfortune, which involved
a six weeks' delay, rather a good thing than
otherwise. Holderness watched Mrs. Winter's expression of these sentiments very
closely, and became convinced of their sincerity. If there was yet no clearly defined
hope in her heart concerning him, at least
there was no fear. At the end of a week he
had persuaded himself that her serious opposi-

tion was not to be dreaded in the fulfilment of his great resolve.

The resolve stood by him now as the one constant companion of his waking hours; figuring likewise in all his dreams, stimulated, thus, by his forced inactivity of body, — by the fact, too, that weeks passed without bringing a favorable moment for its expression. Although he saw Barbara daily, they were never left alone together. He made advances, nevertheless, in the ways that lovers use, — in a stronger pressure of the hand than was needed, in an eager attention to all she said and did. When she was with him, his eyes hardly turned from her; he watched for her coming, and delayed her going by every means he could invent. He often referred to the train hand whom she had befriended, secretly blessing that bygone adventure which had given so good an excuse for praise, direct and indirect; yet grudging the man a tenderness on her part freely manifested then, but certainly wanting now. To be sure, the man had been unconscious, and would never know the debt he owed her. The cases, too, had little in common; the former one was a question of life or death, and the necessity for prompt intervention had thrown her off her guard. Now, her shyness, her reserve, even the unresponsive silence into which she sometimes lapsed, shrinking from her lover's advance, were wholly natural, wholly admirable. She must have guessed his secret, of course. He had intended that she should guess it; and he would remove by all signs in his power any doubt still left in her mind, that she might be fully prepared for a formal declaration when the hour came in which he should pass swiftly from signs to words.

Thanks to Dr. Hardy and to the sound condition of the patient's general health, his recovery was unusually rapid. At the end of three weeks he hobbled across his room on crutches, one of which was already discarded, a week later, when he received letters deploring his absence upon professional grounds, and begging him immediately to fix the date of his return. Then, Holderness quietly neglected his duty. Two days passed, and these letters were still unanswered. He was perfectly well able to travel; he ought, in fact, to be on his way; but he would not stir without knowing what he called his fate; this was a mightier matter than the mere interests of his profession; his case had suddenly turned into a question of life or death, like that of the mangled fireman.

As he sat alone in his room on the afternoon of the second day, the suspense became unbearable, and he saw the folly of prolonging it. That very night he would ask Barbara to be his wife. To do this he must formally request an interview with her, thereby disclosing his secret to the family. But what did that matter, since the secret was an open one? And yet, if he could only come upon her alone by some happy chance! He caught up his crutch, went to the door, opened it and listened. They had all gone their several ways, undoubtedly, lured into the sunshine by the fine autumn weather. The house was absolutely still, — except for the ticking of the hall-clock. Then he remembered that at this hour Barbara must be at school, teaching the village children their first principles of learning and deportment. He crossed the hall to the library, where the sun streamed through

the long western windows upon that agreeable disorder which denotes constant use.
Books and papers were strewn about; and
after Holderness had pulled these over idly,
his glance turned toward the shelf of Balzac
in a corner of the room behind the door. He
smiled, remembering Hardy's allusion to it
in the old days; and was further reminded
of a quotation made by one of the men at
the camp, as they discussed life's philosophy
around the fire. He had doubted its correct-
ness at the time; now, he would prove for his
own satisfaction that he was right. He took
down the volume, laid it upon the nearest
table, opened it, oddly enough, almost at the
desired passage. The cynic of the camp-fire
had the better memory, after all. Here were
the words, in substance precisely as that chance
companion had quoted them : " Man passes
from aversion to love; but when, beginning
with love, he has reached the point of aversion, he returns to love no more."

The statement, already, as it seemed, sufficiently emphatic, was underscored in pencil;
and a corner of the printed page showed that
it must once have been turned down to mark

the place. The book had reopened there, as if of its own accord. Impressed by the coincidence, amused, too, at the thought that these lines, which he had sought to verify, should prove to be possible favorites of his host, Holderness read and re-read them. Then, pondering, he still lingered, with his hand upon the open leaves, when light steps on the veranda interrupted him. It was Barbara, who had taken the shortest way home from school across the fields to the library-window through which she came into the room. She carried an armful of books; and proceeded at once to put them away on one of the farther shelves, singing softly to herself, evidently believing that she was alone. Holderness, half hidden by the door, closed it gently. Here was the opportunity he longed for, suddenly granted him by rare good fortune. That vital question, which had trembled on his lips so often, should be asked now.

At the sound of the closing door the girl turned, saw him, and started back, involuntarily, with an exclamation of mingled surprise and displeasure so definite that Holderness grew vaguely anxious.

"Am I in the way?" he asked. "Why is it that you always shrink from me?"

"I did not mean — I did not know —" stammered Barbara, while her color deepened. "You startled me a little, because — because I thought I was alone."

"I am thankful to find you alone at last," he said, gently. "For I have something to say — something very important, that I must tell you."

"Oh, please —" she protested, putting her hand to her cheek, but immediately withdrawing it, as if the feverishness were not to be borne. Then she tried to speak again, and words failed her.

"You have guessed it, I am sure," he continued; "it has been in my mind so long, — ever since the day when we met in the train, face to face, after all those years; — the day when I took pride in knowing you. At first, I could not understand the feeling; then, when I understood, I did my best to show it in every way but this, and this is harder than I thought. What I have to offer seems, all at once, so little. I am neither great, nor wise, nor strong in anything but that. My only hope is to make you see how honestly I love you, with my whole heart. I want you to be my wife. That is all."

He had drawn nearer while he spoke, but she retreated, widening the space between them. "Oh, no — no!" she murmured, and turned away, with her face hidden in her hands.

"Only that?" he sighed, after a moment of chilling silence. "Can you say nothing else?"

"Nothing," she said firmly, without looking up. "I was afraid of this. Why did you insist? I tried to stop you — "

"But this is horrible. I cannot believe that you mean it, — that you will not even consider — "

"I am sorry to seem unkind. I cannot help it."

Overcome by his disappointment, he made the mistake of reproaching her for this want of feeling. "You force me to envy the poor fireman," he said. "He did not love you, — he was nothing to you, — less than nothing. Yet you treated him more tenderly."

He waited for her answer, but none came;

then, losing his head completely, he made his second mistake, — a fatal one, — in a reference to the past.

"And yet," he went on, wildly, "you loved me once! You said so!"

He took another step toward her, but now she faced him with burning cheeks and flashing eyes.

"How dare you say that?" she cried. "I do not love you — cannot love you!"

"What?" he retorted, desperately. "Have you reached the point of aversion?"

She started as though he had struck her, and turned pale. "The point of aversion!" she repeated; then, catching sight of the open book, understood suddenly his apt allusion. As suddenly, her expression changed; she looked at him indignantly, in perfect self-command. Their eyes met, and he, too, understood. It was she who had found and marked the bitter text in Balzac. With her look, her attitude thus explained upon the instant, hope left him, and he was for the moment overcome by a feeling akin to guilt, — as if he had been detected in the act of reading written words of hers that he was

never meant to see. And she, still silently
indignant, would have swept past him without another word. But, rousing himself, he
stepped between her and the door.

"Let me go!" she said harshly, in a tone
that repelled him. "Don't touch me; don't
speak to me! I could never listen to you
now, — never, even if life depended upon
it." So, brushing by him, she flung wide the
door, and fled from the room.

For a moment he stood half stunned.
Was this Barbara Winter, or was he dreaming? The very walls, still ringing with her
angry speech, looked unfriendly, unfamiliar.
Alas, it was all true! The hospitable scene,
itself, had suffered no change, though he was
driven from it by his own impulse. And the
miserable result might so easily have been
surmised, had he but kept his senses. Blinded
by headstrong passion, foolish in his own con-
ceit, he had mistaken Barbara's coldness for
shyness. Her reserve had been deliberate, in
the nature of a warning. The old affection
had declined, failed altogether, turning at
last into positive dislike. How or why, what
mattered it? She had tried repeatedly, vainly

to show him this. He had forced her to express it in words that would never be recalled. There lay the open book, with its stern judgment, now sternly emphasized. The philosopher spoke truly. She would "return to love no more." He loved her with his whole heart, only to be convinced that with her whole heart she hated him.

His eyes filled with tears, but he held them back; and turned away, leaning heavily upon his crutch, as if he dragged a chain. A moment later, when John Winter burst in upon him, his power of self-control was taxed to the utmost. Yet nothing in his look or manner aroused the smallest suspicion.

"I have tried my strength," said he; "and find not a shadow of excuse for shirking duty a day longer. My letters are very urgent. I must go to-morrow."

In this resolution he persisted, and, leaving Winter Island early the next morning, never saw Barbara again.

With the advance of surgery the world has discovered that a broken heart need no longer prove fatal. Even a compound fracture of that sensitive organ may now be repaired so thoroughly as to defy detection. In due course, Dr. Holderness met his fate for the third time, and triumphed, marrying prudently, to the satisfaction of his friends. But Barbara Winter lived to the last in single-blessedness, beloved and honored throughout her native township, where her benevolence became proverbial. It could not clearly be demonstrated that she was unhappy. Yet she was the last of her race; and when old age came with its inevitable loneliness, strangers wondered sometimes why so lovable a woman had never married. Then the village wiseacres, smiling mysteriously, would shake their heads, and say: " Oh, Barbara met with an early! " — as the quaint New England speech tersely describes love that is unrequited. The statement supported itself by frequent repetition, until it was generally believed; but the details of her romance could never be supplied. "She met with an early!" That remained the long and short of it, and there the matter rested. Not even the oldest inhabitant of Winter Island was wise enough to add another word of explanation.

OUR ACTRESS

OUR ACTRESS

THE junior partner of Markham & Wade, whose Anglo-American banking-house I called "ours" by right of clerkship in it, seemed, at first sight, an uncouth figure, none too prepossessing. When, consigned as I was to his firm, at the tender age of twenty, for my mental and material advancement, I confronted him late one wintry afternoon in the counting-room at Charing Cross, the effect produced upon me was not one of exhilaration. I stood before a sturdy, grizzled Yankee of middle age whose plain features wore an expression grave rather than unkindly. George Wade, however, lacked the gift of graceful compliment; he never gave much thought to conventional amenities; and his greeting of me, as cool and casual as though I had walked in from the next street instead of from the other side of the Atlantic, showed that for the moment, at least, he could not perceive my aspect of the case at all.

His own relation to it preoccupied and
perplexed him. Here was I, a callow youth
of uncertain attainments, an unknown quantity, so to speak, breaking in upon the busiest
hour of his day, when, as it happened, the
senior partner had gone home. My inoppor-
tune arrival presented complications that he
could not consider just then. The disposal
of me was Mr. Markham's affair, rather than
his; and upon Mr. Markham's shoulders he
promptly decided to shift it. That I had
come alone, a stranger, into a strange land,
needing before anything else a word of cordiality, never occurred to him. So, with the
briefest of welcomes, by no means hearty, he
brushed the obstacle from his path, instruct-
ing me to report again in the morning when
Mr. Markham would be on hand. As I
hastily withdrew, he settled down again to
his correspondence; undoubtedly, in five minutes more he had forgotten me altogether.

This is all of our first interview that I can
remember. I recall more vividly my reflections upon it as I passed out into the twilight
to begin life in London. My heart had been
more and more oppressed with the unwonted

grayness of things all the way up from Liverpool, where I had landed in the early morning, and the weight upon it that night grew
all but unsupportable. Mr. Wade's non-
chalance had proved so disappointing that
from a first stage of vexation I passed swiftly
to an antipathy, which, in a very few days,
was dispelled in its turn ; for George Wade's
brusqueness was but superficial, obscuring a
gentle spirit, as acquaintance soon disclosed.
To know him was to understand this and to
like him ; the better the knowledge, the better the liking. I could smile ere long over
that remembrance of first impressions, which,
proverbially, are to be distrusted. The wise
saw of Sheridan's foolish dame about matri-
mony applies equally well to friendship. In
one or the other, 't is safest to begin with a
little aversion.

Unlike Mr. Markham, who was a single
man of restless habits and no fixed abiding-
place, Mr. Wade had become a London
householder, established with his wife and
two small children in Bedford Place near
Russell Square, at the very heart of Blooms-
bury. I soon learned my way thither through

the time-honored quarter of irreproachable
respectability, which often struck me as pe-
culiarly well chosen for his dwelling. Outwardly, all there was grave and grizzled, like
himself. The house stood in a long, mo-
notonous row, indistinguishable by its sooty
frontage from all the rest; yet, within, it
welcomed the visitor at once with a cheery
air of old-fashioned comfort, delightfully
maintained by its guardian spirit. Mrs. Wade,
a New Englander, much younger than her
husband, was plump, rosy, amiable, light-
hearted. Her irregular features had an expressive charm which made them almost
beautiful, though she would have laughed
that idea down at its first suggestion; it was,
surely, the last one upon which she dwelt.
With her quick perception it took her hardly
a moment to discern my imperfect sympathy
with the London vastness; and her own sympathies, aroused immediately, made her seem
like an old friend, even before our discovery that we had many friends in common
at home. I needed no urging to become a
familiar of the household.

Dining there frequently in those dark November days of my acclimation, by the middle of December I could laugh as heartily as the merry hostess herself when occasion warranted. Her outlook upon the world leaned always toward the comic side; and she was quite capable of making fun in church, as children do. Her merriment sometimes overleaped conventional barriers, sweeping all before it, like a tidal wave. Once, as I remember, when Mr. Wade was preparing to say grace according to his invariable custom, some circumstance had annoyed his wife; and her sharp comment upon it continued while the others waited with downcast eyes. Noting the silence, she looked up to catch her husband's reproachful glance. Then, doubly vexed: "Oh, pray away, George!" she cried, irreverently. We were long in recovering from that.

Dolly Wade — her name was Dorothea, but as she liked the affectionate diminutive, it had come into general use among friends — was devoted to her two little girls, souls of discretion, who always appeared at dessert, immaculately dressed, to bid the company good-night with ceremonial courtesy. Their governess had failed them about the date of my arrival, and I was told that the mischance would soon be set right. Next, I heard that a new governess was engaged. With tears in her eyes their anxious parent confided to me the sad history of the prospective incumbent, — a certain Madame Normand, of Canadian origin, formerly well-to-do, whose husband, a Frenchman, had deserted her. She had established relations with the firm in times of prosperity through a comfortable bank-account; and, now that the evil days had fallen, this vacant place in the Wade family offered itself as a means of relief from her embarrassment. She had accepted it willingly, confidently, as Mrs. Wade declared with manifest joy in the triumphant solution of two difficult problems — Madame Normand's and her own — at one stroke. When I came again, a few days before Christmas, I found the new governess already installed, awaiting dinner with the family in the drawing-room.

She was slight, pale, sallow, with thin lips and cold gray eyes. Her years must have been thirty-five at least, and she looked them all.

Almost immediately I was convinced that she not only had encountered the world's buffets, but also had resisted and resented them. It was probably the habit of resentment that gave to her worn features a hardness of expression tending to check the first impulse of sympathy on my part. The signs of suffering were clear enough; those of resignation or of patient endurance were wholly wanting. Her smile was so like a sneer as to be positively unpleasant. She was not a negative person, however, and I thought her interesting; all the more, perhaps, because I saw that she took not the smallest interest in me.

The only guest beside myself, that evening, happened to be an intimate friend of the family, one Herman Carmichael, a comfortable bachelor nearing fifty, who had an office in the City, where he occupied himself with little more than the management of his own property. This was considerable; for, of Scotch descent, he had ever been canny in money matters, like all his tribe. He might tersely be described as a Scot modified by long London residence into something very like a cockney. He was jolly in his disposition, florid in complexion, rotund in figure, boisterous and boyish in his manners, with little trace left in his speech of the ancestral Perthshire dialect.

Mr. Carmichael sat at Mrs. Wade's right, alone upon that side of the table, within easy reach of the whiskey - decanter from which he helped himself at frequent intervals; supplementing its flow with a small torrent of merry jest to the unfeigned delight of his hostess. I, at her left, made for him an eager, joyful listener. His high spirits were contagious, and, as I yielded myself without restraint to their peculiar spell, we were soon in harmony. Before long he twinkled at me across the table, as an intimate friend might have done. I admired the alert mind revealed by his readiness at repartee; his shrewd comments and bits of philosophy, never cynical, but, on the contrary, singularly humane. He displayed a fondness for children, obviously unaffected, unusual in a single man. His references to those of the household, with whom he appeared to be on terms of playful intimacy, were not perfunctory. No wonder that their mother beamed and that their father chuckled.

Meanwhile, nothing of all this served to awaken the new governess from her chilling impassivity. She sat between Mr. Wade and myself, silent when not directly addressed, monosyllabic in her replies, wearing a look of supreme indifference, as though bored to extinction. If Mr. Carmichael was the life of the table, she certainly did her best to be the death of it. In vain he tried to win her over by shafts of wit pleasantly aimed her way; she would not be cajoled. He was obliged to reckon without Madame Normand. To this contingency it appeared that Mrs. Wade had already accustomed herself; for she quietly accepted it as a matter of course, giving not the smallest sign of annoyance, even at moments when to me the icy demeanor of my neighbor was most disconcerting.

Thus, practically four at table instead of five, we proceeded from soup to fish and thence to the saddle of mutton which Mr. Wade carved with a liberal hand. Mr. Carmichael had told us how, in view of the

Christmas holidays, he had stopped on his way up town at Charing Cross, for a stroll through the Lowther Arcade which was then one of the chief toy-markets in London. He had possessed himself of certain small objects, to him infinitely comical, destined for the children's stockings; and he began to produce them in turn from his capacious pockets. A braying donkey, an elastic, distortive mask, a tin acrobat of wondrous activity were soon disposed about his plate to the joy of the feast, excepting only that of its skeleton, — since Madame Normand would not even smile at their antics. He held his master-stroke still in reserve; and stirred by her indifference to try extreme measures, he presently shot out a toy snake, wonderfully lifelike, that wriggled toward her half across the table. The stroke, masterly, indeed, might have been called abnormally successful; for Madame Normand uttered a piercing shriek, and then toppled over in her chair, white and rigid.

Consternation ensued. The practical joker, hastily pocketing his toys, sat helpless, crushed, nearly as white as his victim, while Mr. Wade, making a dive for her, supported her

in his arms. With his wife's assistance she
was borne away into the library behind the
dining-room. Mr. Carmichael and I were left
alone at table, where I tried to console him,
with small effect, until low moans from within
indicated amelioration there and returning
consciousness. These sounds revived him;
and when Mr. Wade came back, shrugging
his shoulders, making light, too, of the whole
matter, the chief guest grew almost cheerful
again. Later, as Mrs. Wade appeared guid-
ing Madame Normand's convalescent footsteps, he sprang up repentant, with apologies
upon his lips; but these were cut short by
a look from his hostess, who permitted
him, nevertheless, to help her make the in-
valid comfortable upon the dining-room sofa.
There, Madame Normand, properly cush-
ioned, reclined in a graceful attitude for the
rest of the evening, since, on her account, it
was thought best to make no move to the
drawing-room; and there I was amazed to
find her transformed, as it were miraculously,
into a figure of gentle amiability. She refused food, to be sure, with a weary and wan
denial; yet in all else she was graciousness

itself, — not receptive, merely, of benefits
conferred, but, likewise, contributing much,
voluntarily, to the welfare of the company.

The children presented themselves at the
usual moment, wondering, round - eyed, at
the way in which we were disposed, but not
questioning. Mr. Carmichael uneasily ven-
tured upon a timid jest framed for their com-
prehension. Whereupon Madame Normand
actually smiled; then — marvel of marvels
— she capped the feeble joke with a livelier
one; and when, dropping curtsies right and
left, her pupils took leave of her for the
night, she kissed them sweetly. After they
were gone, Mr. Carmichael moved up a low
chair and sat at her feet, interchanging plea-
santries with her. Before long, she led the
conversation in a low, musical voice, parry-
ing and thrusting good-humoredly, betraying by her adroitness wide experience of the
world. Even upon me she bestowed flattering attention, when it was my cue to speak.
Here was a change, indeed!

"Jolly nice woman that!" said Mr. Carmichael, when, departing together, we walked
to the corner of the Square arm-in-arm. I

heartily agreed with him, so strong was the last impression she had made. Then, left alone in the murky street, I began to recall, on my homeward way, the Madame Normand of the early evening, and I strove to account for the transformation that she had undergone. What had induced her to make an effort at good behavior, and to persist in it until, little by little, she had charmed us all? Reviewing the circumstances, I was soon forced to conclude that the solution of the mystery lay in gratified vanity. As I interpreted the incident, Madame Normand demanded for herself the centre of the stage; failing that, she had been miserable, consequently morose. By accident or by design, she had gained the coveted distinction. Having set the house on fire, so to speak, she thoroughly enjoyed our dismay, and rose, amid the ruin, like that overworked bird, the fabled phœnix, transfigured, an angelic being. The more I pondered, the surer I became that all the while she had been awaiting an opportunity, and that the metamorphosis, unexpectedly brought about, was really but the culmination of a predetermined scheme.

An interesting figure, truly, if this were the case! But one hardly to be trusted, rather to be watched and feared.

Such mild apprehension as I felt was not on my own account, of course. Clearly, a mere spectator's part was assigned to me; but an attentive one I became, — at first, to little purpose. Madame Normand replied with reassuring suavity to my inquiries about her health at our next meeting; and, when I found an opportunity to compare notes with Mr. Carmichael, he deprecated my cautiously implied suspicions of her double-dealing. Perceiving that he regarded her as an ill-used person, a sufferer through his own thoughtlessness, for which he must make amends, I discreetly changed the subject, and referred to it no more. His treatment of her, thereafter, was marked by what might be called distinguished consideration; under its soothing influence she expanded, — fitfully, for the old disposition lurked beneath the new one, betraying itself at intervals. Madame Normand was improved, but not made over. This might, or might not, support my view of her. I thought that it did so; yet

nothing could be gained by drawing attention
to the unimportant fact. I held my view in
reserve, biding my time.

My visits were repeated often during the
holidays. One afternoon, when I asked for
Mrs. Wade, I was told that she had gone out
for a few moments, leaving word that, if I
called, I was to wait for her in the drawing-
room. I went up, accordingly, to its high, vacant spaces, which occupied the entire width
of the house in front, but at the back narrowed
into a deep alcove, after the manner of old
London drawing-rooms. Heavy curtains at
the intermediate point, where there was no
door, were usually looped back; but, now,
they had been lowered; and behind them
murmurs of childish voices, reading monot-
onously in the French tongue, indicated the
progress of a lesson there. The lamps of the
front room were lighted, and the fire had
been kindled; in the mellow glow I waited
on alone, hearing, but not heeding, the reci-
tation within; until the voice of Madame
Normand, high-pitched and angry, sharply
interrupted it. Something had gone wrong
with the lesson and with her temper; for pre-

sently came another sound, uncommonly like
that of a box on the ear. Again I heard
it; then the curtains parted, and one of the
pupils, retreating from her natural foe, came
halfway into the room, but, at sight of me,
drew back with an exclamation of surprise.
There was a silent interval, during which I
caught a glimpse of the governess, between
the curtains, eyeing me with a malevolent
look. It was but a glimpse, and she could
hardly have been sure that I had seen her;
yet she knew that I had ears, and when she
spoke again, it was in a tone altered much
for the better. Lightly and airily, as if her
excitement were to be taken jocosely, she
hustled the children off by an inner door to
remoter regions. The incident, closing thus,
threw a strong side light upon Madame
Normand's character; but, though stirred to
wrath, I held my peace. It was no part of
my plan to tell tales out of school.

A moment later, Mrs. Wade, returning,
informed me that she was on the lookout
for a new governess.

"What!" said I; "and Madame Normand?"

"She is discontented, and wishes to try another occupation. I am not sorry ; for, between ourselves, the girls hate her. I think I understand why."

I felt sure that I understood, but Mrs. Wade left me no time for comment.

"And what do you think," she pursued, " is the career she has chosen?"

I could not guess.

"The stage! Just fancy that ! Her arrangements are already made."

I gasped for breath. " In whose company ?" I asked.

"'In whose company' ? For what do you take her ? Her own, of course."

"A novice? in London?"

"Yes. The astonishing part of it is, that she has found a manager to make the venture, to take a lease of Sadler's Wells; what's more, a man of means to advance the money, — a backer, so to speak, — 'angel,' I think, is the theatrical term."

Again I gasped. " They have confidence and courage," I remarked ; "and so has she, beside other qualifications. She is something of an actress, certainly, — in private life."

Mrs. Wade laughed. "The snake scene! Yes, I quite agree with you. That was well done; better, indeed, than you imagine."

" How? in what way? Please explain."

" Before doing that, let me tell you who the 'angel' is. That will make my explanation shorter."

To my curiosity, thus cleverly aroused, there swiftly succeeded a suspicion, at which I shivered.

" No; impossible! It is not —"

" Yes, it is."

" Mr. Carmichael!"

" Precisely. Now, what do you say to that?"

" Say? Why, that it's an outrage! She has hoodwinked, infatuated him; something must be done about it."

Mrs. Wade, with a quiet smile, laid her hand upon my shoulder. " Calm your angry passions," she said, soothingly. " You are shrewd and discerning, as I thought; but, oh, my dear Tim Garner, what a boy you are! Nothing can be done about it, now; it has gone too far. She has completely won him over, as she hoped to do from the very

first. You are quite right; he is infatuated,
and it was all a deliberate plot. She has no
more horror of toy-snakes than I have.
Snakes? Why, she is one herself!"

Mrs. Wade was a true woman, if ever such
existed. She, at first all compassion, had
changed her mind with a vengeance. I could
not help laughing outright, not so much at
her expressive statement, as at its evidence
of how far in opposition the pendulum of
her thought had swung.

She laughed, too, then suddenly grew
grave. "It's no joke. They are, all, dread-
fully in earnest. Edwards, the manager, has
taken the theatre for a fortnight, and is
engaging his company. The rehearsals begin next week. I disapprove, and, of course,
agree to help. Miss Agnes Norman, as she
calls herself, is to stay here until after her
début."

"Her *début!* In what?"

"Oh, tragedy! Nothing else would go at
Sadler's Wells. It's an old play. What is its
name? 'Fazio'!"

The historic theatre, remote from fashionable life, after long oblivion was once more

in favor, under the management of Mr. Phelps, who had drawn the town northward and eastward to a classic revival. None the less, I made my facile prophecy of dire failure for the new venture. Phelps, the tragedian of repute, was one thing and Miss Agnes Norman, the unknown quantity, was quite another, as I pointed out. "There will be a brilliant season of one day," I concluded; "with Mr. Carmichael left in the gloaming to draw cheques for all concerned."

Mrs. Wade needed but this hint of the coming storm to veer again.

"Stop!" she cried. "The opening night must be a triumph, if we can make it so. You and I know that she has talent, and there's no harm in calling it genius — beforehand. George and I are going to stand by Herman Carmichael, and so are you! You never can tell about these viperous people. We may have been warming a second Rachel at the nursery-fire without dreaming of it!"

"All up for Carmichael!" I agreed. "Give your orders, General! What am I to do?"

"You are to begin by telling everybody

of the wonderful actress, soon to be billed all over London — "

"At Mr. Carmichael's expense."

"Precisely; pray bear that in mind. You are to clutch your fellow countrymen by the throat, wherever found, and make them stand and deliver. There can be no better *claque* than a house full of Americans, who have paid their money to see a good thing."

"And the three P's?" I asked; "the pit, — the press, — the public?"

"Leave the press to the management; when the stalls sit up, the pit will sit up, too; as for the public, remember Mr. Vanderbilt's word; the public be — "

"Say no more, — it *is!*"

Mrs. Wade, having reduced me to silence, drew a long breath of satisfaction. "There you are!" she went on, summing the matter up; "now, do your part. George is at work already, and so is Mr. Markham. He has enlisted Mrs. Gregory Sterne, of the Haymarket, for advice and material aid. She is a host in herself, with influence at court. If the firm can't make that first night a howling success, it lacks enterprise. The new star is ours now; we endorse her, and our endorsement is not to be taken lightly."

Thereafter, the scheme of patronage to which Markham & Wade stood committed lay at the back of all our minds in waking hours. We met to talk of nothing else, and comparison of notes soon showed that the first performance, at least, would be well attended. The Americans were buying up stalls and boxes rapidly, — "all of a twitter over it," as Mrs. Wade declared. We had led the horses to water; but would they drink?

No shadow of doubt disturbed the two most keenly interested. The star beamed with the lustre of high emprise, gloriously reflected in the satellite. Mr. Carmichael revolved about her in one invariable orbit. He stuffed his pockets for ready reference with newspapers containing every form of preliminary puff or advance notice. Whatever the extravagance, he accepted and quoted it; thus proving himself the ideal angel, an adoring one. There was but a single light in all the firmament for him. His state, in short, was truly deplorable, as I thought at all times and occasionally said, though never in his hearing.

Of course, the immediate effect of these hysteric conditions was to put Madame Normand upon her best behavior. No longer a handmaid in the house, but a pampered guest, she had become the centre of the whole system, in which education, for the moment, had no part. The children, rejoicing in their holiday, discoursed of rehearsals and the wondrous white satin in process of construction for the third act. I caught them one afternoon in a corner of the library, practising a death-fall. For light reading, they had secured a copy of "Fazio." "Demoralizing, isn't it?" whispered Mrs. Wade to me, once, while each member of the family in turn tried on a rope of waxen pearls; "but it will not last. She leaves us the morning after!"

These incidents, trifling in themselves, were impressed upon me strongly from their contrast to those of the daily routine which now had become my second nature. During office hours, occupied as I was in the issuing of drafts and credits, with calculations of exchange and an array of minor details dependent for their disposal upon mental accuracy, little time was left me for casting the horoscope of Madame Normand. I could put her destiny behind me while my desk and its pigeon-holes filled all the foreground; and yet her problem, now ours also, was ever at my back, like black care at the horseman's, quick to assert itself at short notice.

It chanced that supervision of one of our printing departments had been assigned to me. This involved occasional visits to the printer's office in Mark Lane, a stone's throw from the station of the underground railway,— my direct method of conveyance from Charing Cross. I was still young enough in London life to find these hurried flights to and from the City amusing, no matter how dull the weather; sometimes, I prolonged them a little by combining my errand with the luncheon-hour, when, after beef and "bitter" or toasted cheese in a dusky coffee-house, I had a few minutes' leeway for a glimpse of the fog - bound river or some famous landmark of the olden time. My note-book held a list of such memorabilia, compiled chiefly from Dickens, Pepys, and Dr. Johnson, for use in case occasion served.

One dismal Saturday, business and refresh-

ment had been briefly despatched, leaving
me appreciable time to spare. So I turned
off into Hart Street for a look at Saint Olave's
Church, — the church of Pepys. That small
sanctuary, spared in the Great Fire, contains
among other curious relics the tombs of the
noted diarist and his wife. It has come down
to us from the Commonwealth times practically unaltered, hidden away in one of the
darkest corners of the City's heart, to brighten
by its quaint survival gloom that in winter
reeks and clings. The door stood open, and
I found within a cheery sexton, dusting the
old square pews for morning service upon the
morrow. He pointed out the monuments I
sought, but it was clear that he was not one
to hold communion with illustrious shades.
His thoughts were all of his duties toward
the present-day congregation, if such it could
be called. "Oh, yes, they still come," he
said, in answer to my question; "though not
so many now."

He resumed his work, and I went out,
immediately remembering that Pepys once
lived in Seething Lane, on the corner of which
the church stands. I turned the corner, to

make what was to me a thrilling discovery. I stood before one of the "best beloved churchyards" of Dickens, to which, avoiding precise terms of identification, he gives the name of "Saint Ghastly Grim." "A small churchyard," he says of it, "with a ferocious strong-spiked iron gate, like a jail. This gate is ornamented with skulls and cross-bones, larger than the life, wrought in stone; but it likewise came into the mind of Saint Ghastly Grim that to stick iron spikes a-top of the stone skulls, as though they were impaled, would be a pleasant device. Therefore the skulls grin aloft horribly, thrust through and through with iron spears."

Here it all was, just as the great romancer had jotted it down. I gazed at the skulls with the same "attraction of repulsion" that he describes, delighted thus to happen upon a spot for which I might long have searched in vain. The gate was unlocked; I pushed it open, and went in, following up my small adventure. Here and there, among head-stones all awry, grew evergreen shrubs, — poor, sickly things; and as I stooped behind one of these to read the inscription upon a

slab embedded in the scanty earth, I heard
the sound of footsteps and of voices close at
hand. The speakers were a man and a woman in earnest conversation; no startling
matter in itself; and yet I started, recognizing at once the woman's voice as Madame
Normand's.

Directly opposite the gateway, across the
lane, an open door led to a staircase whence the
two figures emerged, to stand for a moment
upon the step absorbed in talk; so deeply that
had I been in plain sight, they would hardly
have perceived my presence, which my shelter left unsuspected. The man, pale, slight,
black-browed and bearded, looked like a foreigner; and their speech was an odd mixture
of tongues wherein French predominated.

"Absurd!" she declared, as they came
out; "*ni l'un, ni l'autre, mon ami!*"

"Ah!" returned the man; "frankly, he
is an idiot, then."

"And if not? If it were one motive, or, indeed, the other, what would that matter after
all, — frankly?"

His reply came in a dialect to me unin-
telligible; but at it she laughed heartily.

" Jealous, eh? Who is the idiot now? I repeat that it is only art he loves. It is for that he pays me money."

" Now, perhaps," he protested; " but how long —"

She interrupted him with an exclamation of contempt, and led the way on, shrugging her shoulders. "Why, as long as I please, as long as he consents. All that may be left to me!"

Continuing their discussion, they moved off down the lane, out of sight and hearing. I heard no more; but I had heard enough to set me thinking. When they were gone, I crossed the narrow lane for a look at the house. Its hallway stood open, and though the ground-floor was given up to offices, a placard in one of the windows announced lodgings to let above. The man, perhaps, lived there.

Who was he? As to that, their talk, frank as it was, kept me in the dark. That seemed, however, to matter little, when its principal theme was clear to me as noonday. The man, — the other man, — whose motives it concerned, their lover of the arts, their source

of supply, could, of course, be none but
Herman Carmichael.

More than ever, thus, the simple Scotch-
man appeared to me an infatuated victim.
Pondering this on my way up from the City,
throughout all that day, indeed, and the next,
I came at last to regard him in the light of
a brand, half-consumed, to be snatched from
the burning. That pious task was hedged
about with difficulties. He had committed
himself, undoubtedly, to certain things ; they
were his business, not mine ; deliberate interference he would surely resent. I must inter-
fere, and yet seem not to do so.

I might have confided in George Wade
and his wife to secure their coöperation; yet
I shrank from this, lest it should give addi-
tional ground for offence. To keep my own
counsel, as I decided, was best, thereby placing
to the credit of the account, when I opened
it, a saving grace of discretion.

The opening came almost of itself, sooner
than I had dared to hope. On Monday morning Mr. Carmichael turned up at the counting-room. By good fortune the partners were
out, and he appealed to me for some trifling

information. When that had been supplied,
I casually introduced the name of our actress,
finding him eager to talk about her. We sat
down in a corner apart, that he might give
me the latest news. All was going well, he
said ; he wished I could follow the rehearsals ; I should find her in splendid form.

"She looks so," I responded, innocently;
"I saw her on Saturday in the city, — Seething Lane, it was."

"Ah! In Seething Lane?"

"Yes; coming out of a house with some
friend of hers, — a foreign man."

"Her press-agent, Morowski, no doubt.
Did you have any talk?"

"No; we did not meet. She never knew
I was there. They did the talking, which
I overheard. I could n't help it."

Thereupon, I blurted out the whole conversation to the best of my remembrance, word
for word, yet lightly, hoping thus to convince
him that this was merely a piece of imprudent
gossip, without *arrière-pensée* on my part.

The scheme worked to perfection. He
would have stopped me at first, but I was
too quick for him; then, attentive in spite

of himself, he heard me out, while his face became a study in varying emotions.

That he writhed with inward rage I could not doubt; for one moment he looked as if he longed to slay me. My innocence disarmed him, however, and suggested a better thing to do. He, too, caught the histrionic mania, which was in the very air around us like an infectious disease. When I had finished, he laughed with a fine assumption of heartiness.

" Ha! Ha! Very good! " said he. " That fellow will have his little joke; I understand it all. By the way, you have n't mentioned this?"

" Certainly not!" I answered; then, by a stupid blunder, almost wrecked my ship in port. " I only felt you ought to know."

His face changed instantly, and, perceiving the danger-signal, I promptly righted the helm: " The joke, you see, was too good to keep."

That saved the day. He laughed again. " Precisely; but we 'll keep it to ourselves." And he went away, still laughing.

His light touch, though admirably conceived and executed, left me unconvinced; afflicted, too, with baffled curiosity as to Morowski and his little joke. The lightness in that respect had been overdone. My curiosity, as I knew, might well be called impertinent; yet I could not shake it off. I had succeeded, however, in conveying a warning without challenge from him or open reproof. So far, so good; after all, there was much satisfaction in that.

The first performance had been fixed for Saturday of the following week. On the day before occurred a full-dress rehearsal, which Mr. Markham attended in company with his influential friend, the distinguished *doyenne* of the profession, Mrs. Gregory Sterne. I knew that Mrs. Wade must also be there, and on Friday afternoon I dropped in at tea-time to hear about it, fortunately finding her alone. The star had been induced to take much-needed rest, — "thoroughly done up," as my hostess declared.

"Well, how did it go?" I asked.

"Of itself! Were my judgment worth anything, I should defy openly your three P's. Mrs. Sterne —"

"She was there, then. What did she say?"

"One thing which impressed me. She said, 'That woman has been on the stage before.'"

"Important, if true! It would account for the woman's courage; yet she invites us to a *début*."

"So we were led to consider it. I can't say that the contrary would altogether surprise me."

"No more can I. The surprise will come when we once detect the lady in telling the truth."

Mrs. Wade laughed. "A little hard upon the lady, that, don't you think?"

"Not at all!" I protested. "That is my tribute to her talent, — genius, if the critics choose to call it so. Your born actress must act all the time, and I'll swear that ours never draws an undramatic breath. Tell me more, please!"

"No, you will see it, yourself, to-morrow, and I repeat that my opinion is good for nothing. Have some tea! All I can say is that it goes."

I could not wring from her another word.

The next morning, — the morning of the day, — Mr. Edwards, the manager, called at the office. He was a thin, careworn man, who looked as if he had never taken a vacation in his life. We had met before, and I recognized at once the estimable figure, which seemed to be inscribed, as it were, with what the French call *succès d'estime*, — triumph, that is, without attendant pecuniary profit. So far as I knew, that kind of success had long been his portion, and remembrance of the fact chilled my feeble enthusiasm for his newest venture. However, he asked for me, producing with the most sanguine air at his command a number of small handbills, which he wished me to distribute about the rooms for the benefit of whom it might concern. I took them, of course; then some fiend prompted me to say : —

"These are Morowski's work, I suppose."

"Mor— who?" he asked, blank and puzzled.

"Morowski; isn't he your press-agent?"

"No; we have none. I attend to all that,

·myself, — to the credit of profit-and-loss account. Who is your foreign friend? I never heard of him."

Who, indeed? A figment of Mr. Carmichael's brain, summoned, on the spur of the moment, to shut me up. I had suspected that at the time, and now felt sure of it. Morowski did not exist. Who, then, was the man of Seething Lane?

We were all acting, through the star's inspiration, and mine was what the wags call a "thinking part." Could thinking alone beget distinction, I should have been leading-man that day.

Sadler's Wells Theatre, heritage of fine tradition, went out of existence so long ago that the very site is now almost forgotten. Its interior was cold and barn-like, according to modern taste, meagre in decoration; yet the pseudo-classic lines had simple grace; moreover, they were not too vast for comfort; one could see and hear anywhere within those dingy walls, which, that night, glowed with color in all their overflowing tiers. We had worked wonders in drawing a brilliant, eager throng to far-off Islington.

Even the sombre Edwards, wearing evening-
dress, with a pink in his button-hole, looked,
as Mrs. Wade said, the incarnation of
gayety.

Seated in a corner of their box, I helped
the Wades to control the children, who were
undergoing a first experience of the theatre.
Long before the curtain rose they grew restlessly ecstatic. When Herman Carmichael
saluted them from the front row of the stalls,
where he sat alone, they shouted for joy; but
the turning-down of the lights subdued them
at once, and when the play began, they followed it with the quiet absorption of trained
theatre-goers.

The grim, conventional tragedy of "Fazio,"
Dean Milman's youthful work, dates from
Byronic times, and has long been consigned
to outer darkness. Its dry bones rattle mildly
in the closet now. One stirs the dust upon
them to smile disdainfully at their hectic
popularity through two generations. Viewed
thus in cold blood, the so-called characters
are merely flat, painted puppets, strung on
wires; but the play's long life was of the
stage, not the closet; and it must be admitted

that the wires are worked with a theatric skill which in the glamour of the footlights lends factitious importance to the strained intrigue.

Fazio is a Tuscan alchemist, seeking the philosopher's stone that shall transmute all things to gold. As he works in his laboratory at dead of night, his neighbor, Bartolo, a miser, is attacked by ruffians, and, flying for help to Fazio, dies in his arms. Fazio, yielding to sudden temptation, steals the dead Bartolo's treasure, and buries the body with the assistance of his wife, Bianca, who thus becomes accessory after the fact in the crime. By foul means the seeker's dream of wealth is realized, and its source goes unsuspected. All prospers with Fazio for a time. Then a rich, unscrupulous favorite of the court, the Marchesa Aldabella, ensnares him; for her, he neglects his wife, who, maddened by jealousy, denounces him to the State. The miser's body is unearthed, and Fazio, accused of murder and robbery, is condemned to death. Bianca, repenting too late, vainly implores his reprieve. The sentence is fulfilled; the desperate Bianca, crazed

by grief, strays in her white satin into a court
festivity to unmask the treacherous Aldabella
and die of a broken heart as the curtain falls.

Such is the artless, romantic tale, technically teeming with "points," that, in the
past, compelled attention to all their turgid,
quavering insincerities. As the leading part
of Bianca is especially rich in them, it became the touchstone, traditionally, of every
successor to Miss O'Neill, its first gifted interpreter; and to these mock heroics, which
then were entirely new to me, I fell that
night an easy victim. Like the children, I
watched and listened breathlessly, — applauded, too, in the proper moments that
came thick and fast at the instigation of the
pit, where manifestly the play was an old
favorite. All was sufficiently well done to
make the action plausible and justify the fervor of the groundlings. With them I accepted
our actress from the first, wondering at her
skill. Though in the earlier scenes her opportunities were few, she was graceful, fair
to look upon, — ten years, at least, younger
than her age. Her voice had a strange, me-
tallic quality, not without charm, at times;

at others, it was soft, musical, with a caressing note; yet always each word detached itself clearly and distinctly. Ease, presence, diction; in five minutes she had proved her command of these requirements, establishing thereby that sympathy with the public which in melodrama is more than half the battle.

At the opening of the third act, Bianca comes fairly to the front. Thenceforward, all woes converge in her. She has but to keep the audience awake, and the thing must play itself, — passably well, at least. With feverish intensity one harrowing scene followed another; she was recalled again and again. Little by little, however, as the night wore on, there crept over me a sense of disappointment. Genius has the inexplicable power to sweep all thought save that of its own greatness from the mind. This woman held me by other means, with a kind of morbid interest, a special wonder in herself, not in Bianca, who never for an instant became real. As in her snake scene of Bedford Place, as with her unknown confederate of Seething Lane, she was acting, always acting, — striving with clever, subtle intent, from motives unrevealed, to gain some hidden end; until, at last, I likened her to one that lurks in ambush, furtive, repellent, artfully counterfeiting truth, when she should simply have been true.

The fact was, perhaps, that I knew a shade too much of her. So far as I could judge, these doubts of mine were not shared by the audience, which at the end applauded generously. Even Mrs. Wade, who certainly had grounds for distrust, seemed hearty in her approval. Had I been ten years older, I should have understood that the favor of a first-night house, packed with allies, is often to be discounted, — taken, as it were, with a grain of salt, even in London. A few moments later, quite by chance, I gained of this an unexpected inkling.

I had parted from the Wade family at the door of their box and walked down the corridor alone. Hardly ten steps off, another box-door flew open, and there appeared upon its threshold the resplendent figure of a woman. Waiting as she passed, I studied her intently; for she had been pointed out to us early in the evening as a Parisian actress of some distinction. The man with her made a com-

ment upon the performance in which I caught
the heroine's name. She smiled, shrugged her
shoulders, and whispered back : " Cabotine ! "

" Cabotine ! " I heard no more, and they
were gone; but I had recognized the harsh,
technical term of the boulevard for a hack
player, tricky, uninspired, mechanical. A
hard word, — so hard that, at first, it seemed
unjust, a jealous one; yet it accorded singularly well with my own prejudice, summing
up my crude impressions, formulating, at last,
my inarticulate utterance. That word and no
other was the word for her : " Cabotine ! "

I slept late the next morning, and when I
woke the boys were already crying the only
Sunday newspaper of that time, " The Observer." Sending out for a copy, I turned at
once to the notice of our first performance.
It proved to be provokingly short, none too
well written, guarded in its tone, which,
upon the whole, was favorable. So far, so
good; but, after all, an " Observer " notice
counted for little. The opinions, really worth
having, would come in the great dailies upon
the morrow.

When these came, they were marked

chiefly by a puzzling lack of agreement.
The only approach to that was negative; for
none of these august arbiters discovered in
the new actress a star of the first magnitude;
none held out to her the hope of fame. Failing this, the numerous judgments recorded
as many degrees of the critical temper. Some
were careful, minute; some negligent and
vague. One found her so dull as to be hopeless; another detected the faults of an old
hand, thoroughly trained in a bad school; a
third fancied in her youthful inexperience
some signs of promise that might or might
not be realized in the remote future. So
these retrospects and predictions drifted in
from day to day, until the artistic weeklies
— one distinctly severe, the other coldly in-
different — set their seals, as it were, upon the
chronicle, closing it for all time.

I dwelt upon the adverse opinions, taking
them too seriously; making no allowance for
the word of mouth that passes from lip to lip
with far more effect upon a theatrical career
than the connoisseur's printed verdict. How
many an aspirant, upheld by popular support,
has stemmed the countercurrent of the press

triumphantly, laughing it to scorn! Mrs.
Wade reminded me of this, as we compared
notes over the tea - table in Bedford Place
when the first week was half over. According to her the houses were holding up, and
the only test of success must be a financial one.
She was radiantly sanguine on that score;
but a part of her radiance was due, as I felt
sure, to the fact that Madame Normand had
been installed in lodgings somewhere near
the theatre. She was rid of her at last; and
no tongue could do justice to all that she had
undergone with a tragic actress quartered
upon the household, which now, happily,
resumed its normal shape. The new governess, a quiet little English girl, was perfection; and the children — bless their hearts!
— behaved already like themselves.

When I mentioned Mr. Carmichael, Mrs.
Wade's face clouded. It was hard, of course,
to have an old friend of the family suddenly
transfer his keenest sympathies to one drawn
completely apart from it. She revealed unconsciously some natural jealousy in the tone
of her remarks about him. The notices, it
appeared, were, in his opinion, outrageously

unjust. He intended to rectify that in some
way,—just how, she did not know; and he
had gone mad over his heroine; desperately
in love, that was the long and short of it;
in a fair way to ruin himself, financially and
otherwise; for, capable now of the wildest
extravagance, he might be expected to run
off with her any day without warning. The
woman had captured him body and soul.

By way of reassuring her, I pointed out
the lack of coherence in these views. "It
takes two to make an elopement, as well as
a quarrel," I suggested; "if she succeeds, her
ambition will prevent that; if success is assured already, as you think, there can be no
financial loss. Her methods are scandalous,
but she does not desire a scandal so much as
public admiration and private comfort; and
you must admit that Mr. Carmichael is old
enough to take care of himself,—a Scotch-
man, too!"

"That's what George says," Mrs. Wade
rejoined; "but Herman Carmichael is be-
witched, and there's no fool like an old fool.
He behaves like a babe in arms. It's all very
well for you to talk; you're not responsible

as I am, since I brought them together. Something awful will surely happen; you'll see!"

She would not be consoled.

The end was beginning even then, although we did not know it; for the houses, liberally enlarged by free tickets, were "holding up" only in appearance. With the opening of the second week, advance sales ceased, and the question of continuing the engagement could no longer be considered. "The jig is up!" George Wade declared, one morning, as he tossed me a handful of passes; "give these to the boys, or put 'em in the fire! I'm sick of the whole business; the show's a good one, but the public does not want it. Edwards frankly owns himself a failure."

That was the melancholy truth. Once more, the ill-starred manager had achieved his customary *succès d'estime*.

Appropriating one of the passes, I journeyed over that evening to Sadler's Wells. It was a chill, drizzling night, into which as I neared Islington a thick fog slowly settled down. The theatre lights, within and without, seemed to burn dimly in the heavy air. At first sight, the audience looked fairly

large, but close inspection showed that the
house had been cleverly "dressed," according to a theatrical phrase; that is, the occupied seats were so scattered as to conceal gaps
and deceive unwatchful eyes. As I went in,
two ushers leaned against the wall, close at
hand, chatting idly. "Mostly snow!" said
one; thus laconically expressing in their dialect the fact that the assembly was in great
part composed of those presenting slips of
white paper, like my own. "Sit anywhere!"
he said, indifferently; and I strolled down into
the back row of stalls, from that isolated
post following the play for some time re-
flectively. It moved on with good effect.
The players, despite the thin house, perhaps
because of it, strove to do their best; and their
pains were well rewarded. Applause genuine
and prolonged rang out from the fog-wreathed
walls. "It *is* a good show!" I thought; "if
only the public were not the public, and
Edwards had been born lucky!"

The manager was nowhere to be discovered; but before long Herman Carmichael
loomed up afar off; not seeing me at first,
so that I half believed I should escape him;

then, in one of the intermissions he established himself at my side. To my surprise he was aggressively cheerful in his talk which dealt only with the excellence of the star. He wanted a listener, and I served in that capacity as well as another; but he made no complaints, no confidences, no demand for sympathy. My responses were quite unnecessary; I doubted whether he heard them.

Suddenly, all this was changed. Just before the curtain rose upon the last act, one of the attendants handed him a note which he read feverishly and, with a muttered curse, crushed in his clenched hand. The act began, and, as it proceeded, I felt that the inscrutable Bianca had never played so well. Others, too, recognized this. The applause redoubled. Joining in it, I turned to my companion for approval; but he had shrunk into himself, and I met only his blank, abstracted look, unmoved by anything so remote as the scene before it. At the end, between us and the swaying curtain, the star came and went with many smiling acknowledgments of a triumph well deserved; and Herman Carmichael, while the audience began slowly to disperse, kept his place rigidly, still drawn apart from us, preoccupied, in painful silence; then, at my touch, he started up and followed me without a word.

Near the door, a blast of the night wind struck us. He shivered, took my arm and I could feel his own tremble. "How cold it is!" he murmured. The drizzle had turned to snow, mingling in grimy heaps with the pavement mud. I caught sight of a hansom, and would have hailed it; but he checked me. "Wait a bit!" said he; "there's a bar at the corner. Have a drop of something, first!"

We crossed the street and went into the "Angel,"—fateful word! where the barmaid greeted him familiarly as an old acquaintance. He ordered brandy: and we sat down at a small table, away from the draught of the swinging doors. After emptying his glass, he drew a long breath; then took from his pocket the crumpled letter and threw it upon the table between us.

"Tim!" he said, addressing me for the first time by the intimate diminutive; "Tim, there is something going on here that I don't understand. It's bad business."

"The performance?" I asked; "yet they never played better."

"Oh, that!" he rejoined, with a shrug. "That's all over. 'The jig is up,' as George says. We ring down and out on Saturday." And he laughed, bitterly.

"What do you mean, then?"

"The woman, Tim; she's playing fast and loose with me. I can't make her out. See here!"

He unfolded the paper, and I read upon it in a rough, pencilled scrawl: "Don't come behind, to-night. Tired out. Will see you to-morrow."

"Well," said I, moved to defend her in spite of myself, "that may be so. Why not? If that is all—"

It was not all, as I well knew. This was but the last straw in a series of equivocal parries and evasions, which he proceeded to demonstrate, then and there. The camel's back had broken, at last; his angelic patience was exhausted, justly, of course. I needed none of his incoherent assurances to convince me.

"She is lying, always lying," he concluded.

"I don't trust her. I'm going to have it out with her,—now!" And he struck the table fiercely with his fist.

I made myself as sympathetic as possible, striving to soothe him; but it would not do.

"Now!" he repeated in the same tone, with the same rough gesture.

"What are you going to do?" I demanded.

"I'm going behind, that's all,—in spite of this!" and he swept away the letter. "And I want you to come with me."

"In Heaven's name, what for?" I cried, aghast. "I shall only be in the way."

"No; I want you there to hear and see,— as a witness!" he explained, laughing grimly. "Come! you must"; he glanced at the clock; "directly, or it will be too late."

I yielded, and was hurried along on his arm, by the darkened theatre, up a filthy side street into a filthier cross-lane. It was snowing hard now; blackened slush, ankle-deep, clogged the pavement as we turned down this passage under a broken gas-lamp in which the flame flickered waywardly. We floundered on toward another light at the farther end gleaming over an archway, which

I assumed to be the stage-door of the theatre. I could perceive dimly through the gloom a four-wheeled cab drawn up before it.

My enforced part in this nocturnal enterprise was most distasteful to me; and yet so curiously does the mind work under pressure of excitement that I became suddenly cheered by the thought of standing for once upon the stage of Sadler's Wells! As we neared the goal, that unlooked-for experience seemed to be one which I should delight in recalling through all my after days.

The happy adventure was never to be mine. Before we had gained the archway, there appeared upon the threshold the cloaked figure of a woman. Then the cab-door opened, and a man leaped out from it. The light shone full upon his face. It was the stranger of Seething Lane.

My companion dashed forward with an oath, confronting them. She never winced, but, smiling sweetly, greeted him in a gentle voice.

"Oh, Mr. Carmichael! Good-evening! Allow me to introduce to you my husband!"

The man, grave, unconcerned, raised his

hat politely; but Herman Carmichael stag-
gered, slipped in the snow, and nearly fell.
Almost before he recovered himself, the pair
had entered the cab and slammed the door.
In the next instant they drove off, leaving us
behind in the wet, amazed, speechless, alone.

We retraced our steps to the "Angel,"
found a cab there, and lurched gloomily
across London to Mr. Carmichael's lodgings in Wimpole Street, saying good-night
at his door. These were almost the only
words exchanged during the long course,
and I saw no more of him for many days.
Our budding intimacy seemed to have been
blighted, for he never confided in me. When
we met again, he avoided even so much as
a reference to that closing scene at the stage-
door of Sadler's Wells. I could only conjecture
how much his theatrical episode had cost him
mentally, morally, materially, and which of
the two "motives" had lured him into it;
or whether it was "*ni l'un, ni l'autre*," according to that emphatic assurance of the
arch-deceiver, spoken for other ears than
mine, yet reaching mine by chance.

That Herman Carmichael did confide subsequently in Mrs. Wade, however, I felt very sure. When I discussed the matter with her, it became clear that she possessed more knowledge thereof than she could conscientiously impart. Though she loved to introduce the dangerous topic, hovering over it like a moth around a flame, in all that most concerned him she was discreet, reticent, yet triumphantly oracular. I am persuaded that she knew to a penny the extent of his financial loss; even the precise nature of his *ignis fatuus*, and through what quagmires and quicksands he had pursued it; but as these were not her secrets she religiously respected them.

Of Madame Normand and her methods Mrs. Wade was ready, nay, eager to talk freely. Bristling with theories of general misconduct, she finally settled down to the belief that we had all been victimized by an adroit conspiracy. She was convinced that Monsieur Normand never really disappeared at all, but had merely changed his address to make his wife an object of compassion and help along the intrigue. My account of the rendezvous in Seething Lane removed her last doubt regarding this. It appeared that the husband

and wife (if such they were) had dined once together in Bedford Place during their apparent prosperity, and that she had found him "an odious little man." She believed them to be a pair of professional adventurers, proficient through long practice, — reprobates, who would stick at nothing.

"What will become of them now?" she wondered. "We shall never set eyes upon them again, you may be sure; but they will go on from bad to worse till they bring up in the Newgate Calendar, I dare say. The distressing thing is that, probably, we shan't know of it."

Thereafter, Mrs. Wade developed a fondness for mapping out the future of these marauders which clung to her for a long time. In two particulars only were her predictions verified. We saw them no more, and we never knew.

Twenty years afterward, I chanced to be in the London of that later date, from which many landmarks had been swept away, — Sadler's Wells and Markham & Wade among them. Even the once familiar Strand was hardly to be recognized. There, in those desert places, I strayed into a new theatre, to see the current fashionable comedy, then at the height of its long run. As I studied my programme before the curtain rose, I started at coming in the cast upon one familiar name, —Miss Agnes Norman! I laughed. "It is impossible, of course," thought I; "a mere coincidence. *She*, like myself, was of a bygone generation." The play began, and for some time the Lady Harrowby of the *dramatis personæ* made no entrance. Then, in the third act, she came on, — an old woman, changed beyond identification, but for her voice. That rang out clear, unaltered, with all its haunting force; there could be no mistaking it.

The part was what is technically known as a "bit"; that is, written for one scene, which required very careful handling. She played it well; so well, that the house all but recalled her. I waited, hoping to see her again; but that was her only opportunity; she did not reappear.

I might have sent in my name, presenting myself at the stage-door for a possible interview; but to what end? That was the end!

Coming slowly out into the night, I thought of my former exit after her *début*, so-called, in " Fazio " ; of my immature judgment ; of the French actress, with her cruel, decisive verdict, long forgotten ; and once more I whispered : " Cabotine ! "

CREDIT AT DUNSTAN'S

CREDIT AT DUNSTAN'S

EVERY householder of the West End knows Dunstan's by name as well as by sight. And even the stranger, lurching down the Strand on the knife-board of his omnibus, looks up at the gray walls of the private bank with an air of respectful familiarity in the very moment of identification. Thereafter, though these walls bear no signboards, they need none for him. He recognizes a monumental importance in that stronghold of financial integrity, standing like a Parisian hotel of the old *régime* between its court and its garden. And there it has stood so long in honorable self-reliance that by common consent the descriptive part of its title has been dropped, leaving it to be known as a possession of the founder, who thus outlives his life two centuries. Not as Dunstan's Bank, but as Dunstan's, pure and simple, does the enterprise to which he committed himself in King William's time main-tain its enviable place among the lesser land-marks of London.

Almost at the beginning of my apprentice-ship with the very young American banking firm of Markham & Wade, I had been sent over to Dunstan's on some trifling errand, — to get an acceptance, probably, — for their bills often passed through our hands; and I have a clear remembrance of the impression then made upon me by the spacious panelled rooms; the green-baize doors, swinging noise-lessly; the mullioned windows, deeply re-cessed, through which, over a gnarled old hawthorn tree, slanted a misty gleam from the Thames. All these appointments had an air of completeness, a time - honored effect indicating perfect fitness of the means to the end, and thus contrasting strangely with our own close quarters, hastily adapted to our needs on a short lease until we could find something better. I knew even then in a gen-eral way of the respect, naturally deeper far than mine, which my employers felt for the peculiar distinction acquired by Dunstan & Co.'s years of irreproachable success. But not until long afterward, when I had been admitted to confidential relations with the partners, did I learn that from their respect had sprung a desire, secretly cherished in the face of mighty obstacles, to turn Dunstan's name and fame to account. My chiefs were energetic Yankees, strong in the faith that overcometh fear, sanguine enough to believe that whatever a man wanted with his whole heart and soul must surely be his at last.

I could not help laughing in my sleeve a little when I discovered their pet ambition, which seemed to me practically hopeless. Yet my discovery was due to the fact that an ambitious dream of my own approached fulfilment. I longed to live in Paris; and thither it was appointed that I should go, to fill what I considered an important post in Markham & Wade's parent house of the rue Saint-Arnaud. There had been vexatious delays, but the date of my departure now stood fixed for the 1st of November. This was only October 5th; yet already I had begun to compute by days the time of durance remaining to me under the autumnal blanket of the fog that hung over Charing Cross. The Boulevard des Italiens had its fog, too, undoubtedly. I knew by experience, however, that life's conditions there were so cheery and bright as to dispel minor grievances of climate. Somehow, in Paris, I never considered the weather at all.

Not so, here. It had rained all day, and I was oppressed by the murkiness of the night as Mr. Markham and I turned out into it from what Gossip Quickly would have called the latter end of a sea-coal fire. Our senior partner was a bachelor, devoted chiefly to the routine of business, over which he often lingered in the private office until his dinner-hour and beyond it. To-day he had called me in for a word about my change of base; the word had led to another and still another; when seven o'clock struck we were deep in talk. Then he had proposed that we should dine together at a queer, old-fashioned chop-house near Temple Bar. So, splashing side by side along the muddy pavement, we passed Dunstan's. My companion glanced up at the dark walls with an expressive sigh, provoked by the train of thought we had been following.

"There's a house for you, Garner!" said

he. "The very air seems impregnated with the spirit of honor and riches."

"What is Dunstan like, I wonder?" was my somewhat inconsequent reply.

"Bless you, my boy, there hasn't been a Dunstan in the firm for these thousand years, more or less. Old Walbrook is the head of the house. I met him, by chance, the other night in the drawing-room of our friend, Mrs. Sterne — at her 'Sunday Evening.'"

"Ah! What was *he* like, then?"

"Quite in character, as Mrs. Sterne might say, if like her he trod the boards at the Haymarket — imposing, inflexible, autocratic — gray-whiskered, with something of a martial air. His unemotional eyes looked through me, but I never flinched. It surprised him, for I heard that he inquired afterward who I was. I did my best to be offish, you see; it is the only way to win him. But it will take years for that, I fear." And again Mr. Markham sighed.

"To win him?" I repeated.

"Yes, my dear Tim, precisely that. He might do an immense deal for us — everything, in fact, by the mere turn of his hand.

Suppose, for instance, that we stood in print as Parisian correspondents on Dunstan's credits. Think of the commissions that would come our way! You will see better what I mean when you get to Paris. And as you are going there, Tim, I don't mind telling you confidentially, that I want just this very thing. I have wanted it a long while, but I can't find my way to accomplish it yet. In the present circumstances I could hardly ask Walbrook such a favor, of course."

"Of course," I gasped.

The calm confession almost took away my breath. That Markham & Wade, young as they were, with a comparatively small capital, could dream of figuring upon Dunstan's credits to the exclusion of older and richer houses was to me inconceivable. Why not wish at once for the Pope's tiara, or even the philosopher's stone?

"No," continued Mr. Markham, more to himself, I fancied, than to me; "were I to ask that now, I should not be answered. Old Walbrook would stare and turn his back upon me. That would be fatal. Nothing kills like indifference. But the hour will come; all I

have to do is to keep my eyes open and to
bide my time."

"The hour will come." Musingly, in a
snug chimney-corner at the Mitre Tavern,
over a clearer fire than our own, Mr. Markham repeated his prophecy more than once
that night. I had never considered him a
dreamer, and this new phase of his character
disturbed me at first. Then, on second thought,
I was properly touched by his confidence.
Does not every man have his hour that will
come, his wild dream unrealized, hidden
away in the sanctuary of his heart from vulgar eyes? To-morrow, at his desk, Mr. Markham would be once more as I knew him,
shrewd, alert, practical. To-night, with sufficient trust in me to relax his guard, he was
thinking aloud. The conditions were pecul-
iarly favorable to such a reverie. We had
dined well, almost by ourselves. For the only
other occupant of the quaint, historic room
happened to be a pale young man with watery
eyes, seated in one of the farther alcoves.
Between the mouthfuls of his frugal meal
he was making notes, apparently, upon some
documents spread out before him. A certain

formality of dress, together with these signs
of industry, suggested to me that he might
be a barrister's clerk, belated in his work, a
part of which, perhaps, he had brought down
from Lincoln's Inn. Whatever the work was,
it engrossed his mind completely. So far as
one could see, he paid no heed either to us or
to the detached phrases of Mr. Markham's
talk that must occasionally have reached his
ears. And before long I forgot that he was
there.

After dinner, we sat in our corner by the
fire until Mr. Markham had finished his
cigar. Then we paid the score, drew on our
overcoats, and made ready for our long tramp
in the rain. While thus we bestirred ourselves,
I perceived that the pale youth was likewise
at the point of departure. Gathering up his
papers, he crossed the room to throw some
crumpled scraps of them into the grate. We
moved toward the door, and had already
passed out when he called us back.

"I beg your pardon," he said; "did not
one of you gentlemen drop this?"

What he returned to me proved to be no
more than a business card of Markham &

Wade, on the back of which I had jotted
some memoranda in pencil. These were of
importance, and I remembered putting them
away in my pocketbook, from which the card
must have fallen to the floor at the moment
of reckoning for our dinner. I explained this
to the stranger in a hurried word and thanked
him. He bowed politely, but nothing more
was said. We went our way, dismissing the
incident as of no significance whatever. Not
for weeks did it occur to me that this bit of
carelessness on my part was probably the link
connecting us with the curious chain of events
that followed.

Our banking-room had an air of its own,
which might be described in general terms
as one of open hospitality. The newspaper
files, the long tables littered with guide-
books, stock-lists, Continental telegrams, and
other sources of useful information, were
available to all comers, new and old alike.
Strangers, as possible customers, were treated
with the utmost civility; and, in consequence,
the place was fast becoming what the firm
desired to make it — a cosmopolitan resort
for the West End of London. There, in a

busy hour, two or three days after my dinner at the Mitre, I was accosted by a man
of good address, who inquired if we dealt in
American securities. Upon my affirmative
answer he produced his card from a leather
case, which seemed to have gone astray in
one of his pockets, for in the effort to find
it he pulled out several letters and a bill of
exchange for twenty-five pounds on a well-
known bank in the City. These, as I observed,
all bore the name upon the card, which gave,
also, his place of abode as Reigate, in Surrey.
The name itself, Arthur Collingwood, puzzled
me ; not from any previous knowledge of it,
but from a conviction that somewhere in
my mind such knowledge must exist, since I
knew the man by sight at least. While he
proceeded to business, which was merely the
conversion of one of our smaller Government
bonds into English money, I tried to identify him, to force an association with his
name — quite unsuccessfully. Nor did his
brief account of himself help me in the smallest degree.

The statement was that he had lately returned from India to his native land, but

that, dreading the severity of its winter climate, he intended to pass six months in the south of France. He might remain at home, perhaps, two or three weeks longer. Could he, without fear of intrusion, make use of our offices during that time? It would be so great a convenience to him that he requested permission to pay for the privilege. I replied, as in duty bound to do, that while a fee was out of the question we should be glad to see him whenever he chose to come. His bond was in order, with all its coupons attached, payable to bearer, perfectly negotiable; I paid for it at the current rate. With a word of thanks he took his leave; and a moment later my sluggish mind awakened to the fact that he was the pale student who had carried his task with him to a dinner of herbs at the Mitre Tavern in Fleet Street.

The fact was not momentous, but it relieved me from that irritating strain which accompanies the mental pursuit of an elusive trifle. On the following morning when Mr. Collingwood called again, I mentioned the circumstances of our first meeting, and found that he, too, remembered them; though until my reminder, as it appeared, he had not identified me. Thenceforward, he turned up every day for one purpose and another, settling himself at our table to write letters or read the morning news. He was amiably inclined to consider his new habit an imposition, for which he wanted in some way to repay us; dwelling so persistently upon this view of the case that I was not unprepared for his subsequent decision to journey into France with our letter of credit in preference to any other. After consultation with me upon the subject, he brought in one day a package of bonds which he desired to sell, covering the issue of his credit with the proceeds.

They were Swedish bonds of the national loan, good securities, undoubtedly, but such as rarely came into the London market; very rarely, indeed, in large lots like this, which was no less than £6000. I found I could not even trace them upon the stock-list; no bonds of the kind had been sold for months. It was impossible, therefore, to fix a price; and explaining the little difficulty to Mr. Collingwood, I suggested that they

should be offered through our stock-brokers
in the City, who would probably obtain a
quotation within a few days. To this Mr.
Collingwood readily assented. I might give
instructions, he said, to sell the bonds for
what they would bring; if in due time they
did not find a purchaser, he would withdraw
them, protecting his credit in some other
way. I handed him, accordingly, a formal
receipt for the securities at their face value,
wrote in his presence an order to the brokers, Messrs. Hallam & Rowles, and went
out with him to the head of the stairs as he
hurried away. I heard the outer door slam
below. It was only our cashier, Wilmot,
coming back from his luncheon. Halfway
up the stairs he met Mr. Collingwood and
eyed him curiously, then turned to watch
the retreating figure. When the door closed
upon him, Wilmot, rushing on, stopped me
with an eager question.

"Who is that chap?" he demanded.

"His name is Collingwood."

"Collingwood — Collingwood? Don't
know it. But I know his face — I've seen
him before."

"Very probably," said I. "He has been here several times."

" No, no, somewhere else ! " returned Wilmot, impatiently. "Several times, do you say ? That 's very odd. What the deuce does he want ? "

"He wants to sell these bonds," I explained. "I must put them away in the safe."

" Yes, yes ; come in here ! " And Wilmot led me into the grated cage, where his duties confined him very closely.

There I transferred the valuable package to his keeping, at the same time communicating the main incidents of Mr. Collingwood's history as related by himself. Jeffrey Wilmot was a keen, sturdy Englishman of thirty-five, with a very clear head, not easily disturbed ; and his unusual excitement over this matter interested me.

"Odd! Very odd!" he kept repeating. "Devilish odd, I must say. Why does he bring them to us? Why does he come here at all, Garner, tell me that ? Blessed if I can see! He is — or was — a clerk at Dunstan's."

"Nonsense! That's impossible."

"Well, I'm as sure of it as — as I am of anything."

Then for a moment in silence we stared at each other with reflective eyes. If Wilmot was right, why should the man seek us out when he had all Dunstan's experience at his back? Why turn from his natural friends to deal with strangers?

"It can't be," I persisted; "or, if it is, he has quarrelled with Dunstan's, that's all."

"Yes, on his way home from India!" said Wilmot, with a sarcastic smile gleaming through his brown beard. "It won't do, Garner; it won't do."

It would not do at all, as I was forced to admit. The clerkship at Dunstan's and the life in India, conflicting hopelessly, silenced me once more.

"There's mischief at the bottom of this, or I'm no sinner," Wilmot continued. "Wait a bit, and I'll prove it to you in five minutes. Hand me my hat, please; now my umbrella. Thank you."

"Where are you going?" I asked.

"Just over to Dunstan's for a little talk. My people kept an account there once, and

I've met old Walbrook. I'll have this out with him, and convince you."

By that time I had come round to Mr. Collingwood's side, convincing myself that Wilmot, misled by a chance resemblance, scented mischief where none existed.

"Good luck!" said I. "But it's all a mistake. I'll bet you a sovereign that you come back without a shadow of proof to stand on."

"Done!" cried Wilmot, pulling out the coin and slapping it down upon the counter. "For two, if you like!"

"No," I laughed, laying my gold-piece beside his; "one will do."

When he was gone, I stowed away the bonds; then waited in the cage for his return. His assistant, one of the junior clerks, had overheard our talk; and in the pauses of work he discussed the problem with me, approving emphatically my final opinion. Our friend Wilmot was cocksure of things always. We both felt a sneaking satisfaction at the prospect of a minute flaw in his infallibility.

In a quarter of an hour Wilmot reappeared.

"Well?" I asked, reading my answer in

his face before he spoke. He had proved nothing; the stakes were mine, as he acknowledged. What had happened, then, at Dunstan's? Had he told his tale? Or had Walbrook simply refused to see him?

"The old bear!" growled Wilmot, angrily. "He would hardly listen. My visit, evidently, was a great piece of impertinence. He never dealt in Swedish bonds, never heard of Collingwood. Nothing at Dunstan's could possibly have gone wrong in the way I suggested. Oh, no, of course not! Their system is perfect over there; suns rise and set by it. Well, thank goodness, I've done my duty! Old Walbrook may go to the devil as soon as he likes—yes, and Dunstan's too!"

When we had chaffed him into good nature, I decided that the whole matter must immediately be laid before the firm—or, rather, before the senior partner, as Mr. Wade at that time was in Paris. Wilmot went in with me; and he was flattered, as I could see, by the chief's attention to his share of the testimony. Yet I also saw that Mr. Markham privately agreed with me in believing the case to be one of mistaken identity. The orders he gave us were to proceed with the sale of the bonds through the brokers; but, when Mr. Collingwood called, on no account to let him go without meeting one of the partners; above all, to pay him no money until such a meeting had taken place. Simple orders and explicit; the obstacles between us and their execution were not of our making.

The first obstacle presented itself in the report of Messrs. Hallam & Rowles, who, after forty-eight hours' delay, wrote that "Swedes," as they called them, seemed to be positive drugs in the market. While the investment was undeniably sound, no one at the moment wanted to go in for it to the extent of £6000. We answered that, so far as our knowledge went, the owner of the bonds was in no hurry to sell them. The order, therefore, might hold over until countermanded. If anything came of it, well and good; if not, after a reasonable time it should be formally cancelled. Meanwhile Wilmot and I awaited with impatience Mr. Collingwood's next visit. Wilmot, because he wished, as he said, for one good look at the man; I, from a presentiment that something of importance, for or against him, must develop in the proposed interview with the chief. But the third day passed, and the fourth, with no sign of Mr. Collingwood. It seemed as if Mr. Markham's second command were even more futile than the first.

"The man's afraid to come," Wilmot declared; "knows me, probably, and knows that I know him. Do you see?"

I laughed at his obstinacy. Then, early on the fifth morning, I showed him a note, addressed to me, just handed in by a messenger.

It was of that date, written at Maurigy's Hotel in Regent Street; and it contained six lines from Mr. Collingwood to the effect that he had been very busy, and, now unexpectedly summoned to Paris for a day or two, was on the point of leaving by the tidal train. If his bonds were sold, the account might be sent to him in care of our Paris house; otherwise I need not write, as he would call upon me the moment he returned. All this seemed plausible enough. But Jeffrey Wilmot did not find it so.

"What's Collingwood doing at Maurigy's?" he asked. "I thought he lived in Reigate."

Again I laughed. "My dear fellow, he stopped in London overnight, I suppose; and why should n't he? The tidal train has gone. He is n't at Maurigy's now."

"I 'm not so sure of that. Where 's the messenger?"

"He went away at once, saying that there was 'no answer.'"

"'No answer,' eh? Well, send one, all the same; it can't do any harm. Write a line of acknowledgment, and give it to me. I'll take it over to Maurigy's. We may discover something. Who knows?"

So Wilmot rattled off in a cab with my note, which he returned to me unopened at the end of half an hour.

"Mr. Collingwood was out, then?" I said, with affected simplicity.

He ignored the underlying malice and only growled in answer: "Left, this morning, with all his luggage."

"What? You discovered nothing?"

"Quite the reverse. I discovered that he

has been at Maurigy's three weeks. What do
you make of that, Tim ? "

" Why, that he prefers the town to the
country — no more."

" Yet the address he gave you was Reigate.
A slippery piece of business. That is not his
address at all."

" Easily said, and easily proved or dis-
proved. Why not take the next train for
Reigate ? or send an inspector down from
Scotland Yard ? "

" Exactly. Why not ? " agreed Wilmot,
with the utmost gravity. " Let us have a
talk about that with Mr. Markham."

This time it was easy to see that the weight
of the chief's judgment leaned Wilmot's way
rather than mine. He felt, however, that to
call in the police would be scarcely worth
while just then. Especially, as in the course
of our conference one of us remembered that
the book-keeper, Mr. Flack, lived at Redhill,
very near Reigate. Flack, to be sure, was a
simple-minded soul ; the last one in all the
world, perhaps, to rely upon for detective
duty. But here the duty involved no more
than a straightforward inquiry which any

tradesman in the town could answer. Should the information received prove unsatisfactory, Wilmot, as Mr. Markham hinted, might have his *carte blanche*, with all the acumen of Scotland Yard behind him.

Beaming with cheerful importance, Mr. Flack reviewed the next morning before our council of three his experiences at Reigate. The Collingwoods, as it appeared, owned a small estate within a mile of the town. But the house had been closed for some time in the absence of the family abroad. The family comprised the master and mistress, well on in years, and one unmarried son named Arthur — presumably our business acquaintance. These facts, ascertained without difficulty at the station, had been confirmed at one or two of the principal shops. And — and that was all. So far as that went, it tended to allay suspicion. The wavering balance dropped back on my side, and Mr. Markham promptly decided that our course must be to watch and wait patiently. With this decision Jeffrey Wilmot was forced to content himself. Upon its announcement, he protested only by a shrug of the shoulders. But afterward in an aside to me, he emphasized the small conflicting circumstance of Mr. Collingwood's omission to give us his London address — a bit of carelessness so marked that it must have been intentional. I, on the contrary, thought the mistake, if mistake it were, entirely natural, since Mr. Collingwood really lived at Reigate.

"Reigate be blowed!" grumbled Wilmot, as we turned to the day's work again. "He does n't live there — he has never lived there! I don't believe a word of it; I don't believe that his name is Collingwood; but I do believe that he's a liar and a damned rascal!"

Several days went by, during which the case stood thus without further development, unless the postscript of a letter from the Paris house could be called one. By this we were informed, in response to our inquiry, that Mr. Collingwood had not turned up in the rue Saint-Arnaud.

Meanwhile, we in London still awaited his return, and the order to sell the "Swedes" remained uncancelled with our brokers, who reported no offer. More important affairs crowded this into the limbo of unfinished business ; Wilmot and I ceased to discuss it; I, indeed, almost ceased to think of it, preoccupied as I was with preparations for my removal to Paris. Besides my daily routine at the office, there were social duties to be despatched. Common courtesy obliged me to take a more or less formal leave of my London friends ; and among these by no means the least was the one to whom Mr. Markham had referred on the night of our dinner at the Mitre — Mrs. Gregory Sterne.

This congenial spirit, conspicuous in public as the duenna of the Haymarket Theatre, whose artistic skill never failed her, held in private a position still more enviable. Her small house just out of Portland Place was, to quote a descriptive phrase then often repeated, a rendezvous for the upper half of intellectual London — drawn thither by exceptional qualities distinguishing the hostess. Never, perhaps, in all the world were sixty years worn more gracefully, more lightly. She had fluent speech and a ready wit restrained by the finest sense of proportion ; guided, too, by a warm heart that, in spite of sorrows, still retained its youthful buoy-

ancy. She could be gay and sympathetic at
the same time, without revealing that under-
current of egotism which so often dims the
shining lights of the stage when we see them
unprofessionally. Mrs. Sterne, in short, was
unaffected, direct, genuine; no one could
make her acquaintance without wishing to
know her better. We had been thrown together in Switzerland, where circumstances
speedily combined to bring about an intimacy, outlasting by good fortune our term
of holiday. The difference in our ages, undoubtedly, helped me in this. For Mrs.
Sterne took a very strong interest in youth,
with its aspirations, its immature judgments
and perplexities. The young kept her young,
as she declared.

On Sunday evening she was always at home,
and as the day drew near I planned my parting visit. Then came a note from her con-
firming the plan, but improving upon it. " I
hope you have me in mind," she wrote,
" and will remember that I count upon you.
This being the case, will you not give me
a little more of your precious time, dining
here early, at seven, before the crowd de-

scends upon us? I want you to meet my *protégée*, Margaret Leigh, who has just become engaged and is to leave the stage; she will dine here with her *fiancé*— you will make the fourth at table. Please come!"

I said "yes" instantly, congratulating myself upon forming one of the *partie carrée*; particularly, because of my desire to know Miss Leigh, whom I had once seen across the footlights. Mrs. Sterne had described her to me as the daughter of an old friend in reduced circumstances, unusually well qualified for the trying career she had chosen. Success in a round of parts had confirmed the judgment; the day was won, the future promised much; but now all would be cut short abruptly. I fancied that I could read regret between the lines of Mrs. Sterne's note. To her the sudden change in Miss Leigh's fortunes must be in some measure a disappointment.

It was this feeling which brought me to Mrs. Sterne's drawing-room a few minutes before the time appointed on that Sunday evening, eager to have as soon as possible an expression of her views. These were not long in coming to the surface.

"Isn't it too discouraging?" she began. "I have toiled and slaved to bring out Margaret's talent, which is really quite extraordinary. I have drilled the poor child to death — for nothing. My time is lost, and the stage loses incalculably. In two years more she would have been at the top."

"But if she is happy now —"

"Happy! Oh, of course, they all are *now!* But I have an eye to the future. I believe that hers would be the happier for marrying a poorer man and keeping on with her profession."

"The man is rich, then?"

"Sufficiently so — they are to travel on the Continent," sighed Mrs. Sterne, as if she were dealing with a grave misfortune. I smiled; then suddenly perceiving the ludicrous side of her complaint, she laughed, and continued lightly : "Ah, well, I must give them my blessing, I suppose. It appears that he is amiable, of good family, and all that. There is really no fault to be found with the match, except that it came about upon short acquaintance. They met at Brighton, and were engaged in three days. Don't look so astonished. That often happens with us, you know; we are less deliberate than you Americans; we *fall* in love, literally."

"Three days!" I repeated. "That was sharp work. Who on earth is he?"

But at that moment came a stir in the hall, to warn us of the arriving guests.

"Hush!" she said. "They are here."

And the servant, appearing, announced:—

"Miss Leigh — Mr. Collingwood!"

In the waiting time that followed our formal greetings, he moved to my side and gave me his hand cordially.

"An unexpected pleasure," I said, awkwardly. "I thought you were in Paris."

"And so I was," he explained. "I arrived back an hour ago. By the way, those bonds of mine — they are sold?"

"No, we are still without an offer."

"It's of no consequence," he replied, passing from the subject carelessly. "I will call upon you in the Strand — to-morrow."

I bowed, groping for words, but not finding them. Just then we were summoned to dinner, and I was glad of the interruption. Taken aback by the new relation with him, which had developed so unexpectedly, I was beginning to distrust Mr. Collingwood. My mind suddenly clouded with those suspicions of Jeffrey Wilmot, now not to be dispelled.

I sat opposite to him at the table, where, while he devoted himself to the hostess, I could study his face without appearing to do so. I found nothing distinguished in it— nothing distinctive except its lack of color; an effect due rather to the peculiar light blue of his eyes than to the pallor of his complexion. In voice and demeanor he was entirely conventional. Yet my impressions were all negative; and I failed to see how a talented, ambitious girl like Miss Leigh could sacrifice her whole artistic future to a commonplace young man whom she had known three days. Surely, the force of love never went farther, I thought; or is it that she has no real feeling for her art at all? And I deliberately turned the talk to the stage, soon discovering that her interest therein remained of the keenest sort. She it was, now, who talked of things theatrical with enthusiasm.

"And yet," I said, with a cautious glance across the table to make sure that we were not overheard; "and yet you hold all this so lightly; it is over; you have dismissed it in a single word."

" Don't be too certain of that," she answered, lowering her voice. " We go abroad at first; Mr. Collingwood wishes it, and I let him have his way. But we shall come back. Then there will be more ways than one; and a woman, you know, always has hers at last."

" Oh," returned I, "if it is merely a leave of absence, not a final renunciation, I congratulate very heartily ourselves, Mr. Collingwood, and you."

She smiled, and nodded. Then the others broke in upon our small exchange of confidences, which yielded to a flow of general talk. Some one spoke of India, whereupon Mr. Collingwood discoursed for a time, while we, who knew nothing of the life there, either listened or led him on with an occasional question. He talked glibly and well; yet I noticed a ringing hardness in his tone which made me positively dislike him. I can see now that the source of this new feeling was probably the jealousy natural to mankind.

I liked Miss Leigh, and he had captured her. But I did not then account for the cause, even to myself; I only fostered the dislike by doubting if she would find it an easy matter, when the honeymoon was over, to have her way with this man.

When coffee and cigars came, Mrs. Sterne, who detested formality, asked if the smokers would really be happier by themselves. One of them, at least, was only too happy to take this broad hint, and the result was that the hostess, with Miss Leigh, stayed by us at the table. The pleasant after-dinner time sped on swiftly, and Mrs. Sterne could have kept no note of it; for, suddenly, the servant made an announcement to her in an undertone. He spoke on Mr. Collingwood's side of the table, and I caught no name; but I understood that the reception - hour had overtaken us, and that there was a guest in the drawing-room. With a cry of dismay Mrs. Sterne started up ; we were all on our feet at once. Then the cry was sharply echoed by Mr. Collingwood, who, clapping his handker-chief to his face, dashed out of the room by a service - door leading to the pantry. The

servant, following him, showed more presence of mind than the rest of us, who were
left staring at one another in blank alarm. Before we could recover, the man reappeared
with a faint smile on his decorous, shaven
face.

"It is nothing, mum," he said. "The
gentleman has the nose-bleed, if you please,
mum, that's all."

"Oh," laughed Mrs. Sterne, hysterically
relieved. "Will you take charge of him,
Mr. Garner, please? Come, Margaret, come
with me. Mr. Walbrook is in the drawing-
room."

We laughed, all three, and I was left alone.
"Old Walbrook! It is he!" thought I;
"of course; Mr. Markham met him here;
no doubt he often comes." So this was the
impressive name that I had failed to catch.
I wondered whether Mr. Collingwood had
caught it. Then, with my hand on the pantry door, I stopped, while a new wonder
overcame me. Was the name so impressive
as to bring on a nose-bleed in Mr. Collingwood's sensitive organism? Was there some
special cause for this effect? Suspicions, again!

Was it not rather Jeffrey Wilmot's obstinacy
that thus, out of a pure coincidence, sought
to forge a new, intangible link between the
guileless Collingwood and Dunstan's?

I pushed open the door, and saw him
bent over the running water, at which he
splashed violently, while the servant stood
by, shrugging his shoulders in a vain effort to
be of use. When I spoke, Mr. Collingwood
neither turned nor looked up, but in a tone
of annoyance bade me join the ladies, adding
that his trouble was not serious, and that he
would follow us presently. I could only leave
him, therefore, and make my favorable report of his condition in the drawing-room.
There I immediately underwent a formal
presentation to Mr. Walbrook, who, barely
acknowledging my existence, addressed himself to more important guests. The room was
already filling up; and while I talked with
Miss Leigh, her uneasy glance toward the
door at each new arrival did not escape me.
Then my attention was distracted, and when
I turned her way again she was gone. But
a moment later I saw her face among the
others, with undisguised anxiety in it. She

hurried across the room to Mrs. Sterne, and, after a whispered word, moved gently away, out at the door. Thereupon, Mrs. Sterne's eye caught mine, bringing me to her side instantly.

"Will you help Margaret to her carriage, please ?" she said. "That is all."

"What do you mean? Mr. Collingwood—"

" He has left the house without a word to her or to any one. Miss Leigh is naturally disturbed and is going home. If you —"

Mrs. Sterne was called off, and I hurried into the hall to find that Miss Leigh's carriage had come up. As I went down the steps with her she seemed bewildered — unaware, indeed, of my presence. But when I asked what orders were to be given the coachman, she came to herself, thanked me, and said he must drive directly home. Then, leaning from the carriage window, she countermanded this.

"No! Tell him to drive first to Maurigy's." And she was whirled away.

Coming back, I questioned the servant in detail concerning Mr. Collingwood's abrupt departure. What had happened? Had he

grown worse, or better? Was he too ill to
speak that he had left no word?

The answer puzzled me. "He seemed all
shaken up, sir, he did," said the man; "un-
easy-like in his mind, and most anxious to
get away without troubling the ladies—
they was n't to know. His nose had stopped
bleeding, sir, but his hand—"

"His hand!" I repeated.

"Yes, sir. He had cut one of his fingers,
sir, which was a-bleeding away, sir, quite
fast. His handkerchief was twisted round it.
I can't think how it happened, sir, for they
was only the silver fruit-knives left, sir, on
the table. It seemed a bit odd, sir, to me, so
it did!"

A bit odd, indeed, I found it. But I kept
my reflections to myself, and made no mention of the supplementary accident when
Mrs. Sterne cross-questioned me a few minutes later. An hour afterward, in taking leave,
I strove to set aside her doubts by informing
her of my business appointment with Mr.
Collingwood for the next morning; a shock-
ing piece of disingenuousness, this, in view
of my strong premonition that the appoint-

ment would not be kept — a premonition
duly verified.

On Tuesday Mrs. Sterne drove up to our
door in a tremulous state, which was intensified by my lack of news. From her I learned
that Miss Leigh had stopped at Maurigy's on
Sunday evening, but had not found Mr. Collingwood. They knew nothing of him there,
though that was always his abiding-place
when he came up to town. Miss Leigh had
then despatched a telegram to him at Reigate
— in vain ; no answer had been received. A
second telegram sent to Paris, *Poste-Restante*,
where she had last addressed him, likewise
remained unanswered. He seemed to have
vanished completely from human ken. What
did it mean ?

It meant, as we feared, but one thing —
namely, a flight. But we had no clue to his motive, and conjecture was idle. Mrs. Sterne drew
the worst conclusions, and went away talking
incoherently of detectives, in case nothing was
heard of the man within the next twenty-
four hours. Nothing would be, she declared ;
we had seen and heard the last of him !
And with the opinion mine heartily agreed.

The opinion, however, was not supported by fact. For, on the following morning, up drove Mrs. Sterne again, to tell me that Mr. Collingwood was in Paris, whence he had written to Miss Leigh a tissue of vague excuses. Business complications had called him suddenly across the Channel, and would detain him there indefinitely. If he was ill, he did not mention it; and he carefully omitted any reference to the precise place of his abode. His address remained *Poste - Restante*. And yet with astounding impudence he begged Miss Leigh, in the view of these same " complications," to join him in Paris, and there to be married quietly with as little ceremony as possible. To what order of beings did the man belong?

"Was there ever such effrontery?" continued Mrs. Sterne, almost in tears. " Margaret to go to Paris! Does he expect her to marry him at the General Post-Office? I think we are dealing with a madman."

" She will not answer that, I hope," said I.

" No, indeed ! " replied Mrs. Sterne, indignantly. " I have already answered it myself in the third person, simply stating that Miss

Leigh declines to recognize him further unless he should present himself in London immediately, with a full explanation. He will not come. What an escape for her! As I said before, he is crazy, of course."

And once more we agreed.

Mr. Collingwood's written appeal served thus but to make what seemed the impenetrable mystery of his proceedings doubly dark. But with mysteries, as with the night, the darkest hour is apt to come just before the dawn. And only three days later the dawn broke, bringing floods of light upon what passed into the annals of Markham & Wade as "the Collingwood affair." It was no less a person than old Walbrook who supplied the missing clue, which tended, first of all, to his own discomfiture; but an old Walbrook humbled and repentant, changed in his behavior almost beyond recognition. Pale, with drawn features, he rushed frantically in upon Jeffrey Wilmot, imploring data to identify the person of whom they had spoken at their last interview; Collingwood was the person's name, he believed. Then Wilmot, in tranquil dignity that was truly magnificent,

reminded the old bear that he had disclaimed
all knowledge of such a person; turning the
barbed weapon of his own indifference in
what was plainly an open wound with so
much skill that Mr. Walbrook flushed to
his temples, and stammered profuse apologies
for past rudeness. Then the scene changed to
our private office, where Mr. Markham, attended by Wilmot and myself as silent sup-
porters, received the excited manager of
Dunstan's with just the right degree of lan-
guid interest. Never was a dramatic situation
more deftly handled. We had the victim
writhing at our feet, and we were triumphant
— but not unbecomingly so.

"I have now reason to suspect that Collingwood is not this man's name," asserted
Mr. Walbrook. "Have you anything to
justify my suspicion? Any signature? Any
scrap of his handwriting?"

We had, of course, on file the short note
addressed to me from Maurigy's; and this
was produced forthwith. At sight of it Mr.
Walbrook turned almost livid.

"Yes, that is he! No doubt — no doubt!"
he gasped.

"He! Who? Who is the man?" asked Mr. Markham, with genuine sympathy.

"He is a thief and a scoundrel!" replied old Walbrook, dropping back in his chair and gaining, as he went on, unnatural calmness. "That is the handwriting of Thomas Watts, my former bond-clerk. I can tell you his story in a very few words. He is of excellent family connections, the son of a clergyman at Redhill, and he was in our employ a long time. For ten years, at least, we have trusted him with everything. But two months ago, on the ground of ill-health, he resigned his post, intending, as he said, to try a southern climate—to leave England. Yet he had saved little, and must earn his livelihood. In view of that, I gave him a letter—a very strong letter —of recommendation. Yes, I did this! And he—"

Here Mr. Walbrook drew a long breath and laughed bitterly.

"I understand," said Mr. Markham. "He robbed you."

"No," said the manager of Dunstan's, recovering himself. "That would have been difficult, if not impossible. He did better.

You understand, of course, that we have many
depositors who leave in our hands their securities, which are often payable to bearer, for
collection of the interest. As the coupons
fall due, we cut them off and credit the sum
to the owner's account. Watts took charge
of this; and it was done promptly and accu-
rately as usual on the last quarter-day. Then
he possessed himself of such available bonds
as he saw fit, storing away with the utmost
care the empty envelopes. When his nest was
comfortably feathered, the ill-health and the
warm climate followed easily. We have not
yet determined the full extent of the loss,
which undoubtedly includes those 'Swedes'
of yours. You have not sold them?"

I reassured him. The Swedish bonds were
still in our safe, unsold.

"For a new hand, the fellow is adroit,"
said Mr. Markham. "He plays the game
well."

"Well!" repeated old Walbrook. "Like
a master! But for an accident, even now I
should not have suspected him. The natural
date of discovery fell on the next coupon-day
— November 1st. His game was so well

planned that he could play it at his leisure. And now—where is he?"

This question I strove to answer by describing Mrs. Sterne's dinner-party and what followed it, including the collateral evidence drawn from her expeditions to the Strand. Mr. Walbrook was much interested in the little scene over the walnuts and the wine. Clearly, the criminal had "read up" India for use at such a time; and had attached himself to the respectable Reigate family because he knew that every member thereof was in a remote part of the world. Clearly, too, catching his employer's name, he had taken the alarm and, driven to desperation, had feigned hemorrhage on the spur of the moment; a little later, probably, to give it the semblance of color in case of inconvenient sympathy, he had slashed his hand. The inevitable hour of detection was very near. And we concluded that under the strain of his anxiety he had chosen the wiser course of awaiting it across the Channel. And now—where was he? All came back to that in the end, which left but one answer possible. For the moment, at least, he was out of reach.

The interview closed with Mr. Markham's agreement to hand over the Swedish bonds to Dunstan's, upon receipt of their written pledge to hold us harmless in the improbable event of disputed ownership. When Mr. Walbrook acquired them, a few days later, by means of this formal document, he could not say too much in praise of what he was pleased to call our discretion. He wished, indeed, for the power to make some adequate return for it. Here was Mr. Markham's opportunity. Without a moment's hesitation he expressed his long-cherished desire to figure in print upon old Walbrook's credits. His hour had come. From that day forward, upon no ground that the world could discover, the new house of Markham & Wade, much to its advantage, was registered as Parisian correspondent of Dunstan's.

We heard no more of the cunning thief, and, so far as I know, he was never brought to justice. As time went on, I complained to Jeffrey Wilmot that the vaunted skill of Scotland Yard seemed for once pathetically impotent. He stared at me with wondering scorn.

"My dear boy, Scotland Yard has never been called in, of course. Do you suppose old Walbrook is so dull as to submit that affair to the tender mercies of the public? Why, Dunstan's never would get over it! He has simply made up his loss like a man, and swallowed the bitter pill. The last thing on earth he wants is to clap his hand upon your Collingwood, Watts, or whatever the name may be!"

There was reason in this—the same reason which always kept that undetermined "full extent" of Dunstan's loss from our knowledge. By great good luck we had restored £6000 of it; but the sum total of the missing remnant has never been revealed.

To Mrs. Sterne's joy her pupil soon returned to the stage. She is the same Miss Leigh who, fulfilling her early promise, held so long the world's attention; and then, marrying happily, passed into retirement, rich in accumulated fortune and in fame—alas, like all fame possible to the player, already waning!

Thus ended "the Collingwood affair," so long ago that to-day it is, perhaps, entirely forgotten even by its victims. Though, for years, one or two of us found it frequently a subject of fruitful comment and speculation. Our jovial, simple-hearted Mr. Flack, especially, was never tired of alluding to it; for a special grievance, arising from his slender share in this peculiar case, oppressed his mind.

"To think," he would say, "only to think that I went out of my way a-looking up Tommy Watts — Tommy Watts, of Redhill, that I've known the whole of his blessed, blarsted little life — and never knew it was him I was a-looking for!"

THE PENGUIN

THE PENGUIN

STRANGELY enough, I had never dreamed that George Wade possessed a voice. Not that, as junior partner of Markham & Wade, he would have been at all likely to break into song during business hours at his banking - office of the Strand, where, daily, I stood under him; but I had dined often at his house in Bedford Place, and his hospitable wife always did her best to make me feel at home there. Sometimes, I found her at the piano; for she played a little, herself; constantly, too, she considered some question of the children's lessons. Under his own roof-tree, not unreasonably his accomplishment in music might have been hinted, to say the least; yet I could recall no such disclosure. I should have as soon suspected the hard-headed practical man of versifying as of singing a ballad.

Under Mr. Markham's wing I had been stationed for some months in the Paris house. Midsummer had come, bringing with it days

of comparative repose; and the senior partner had gone over to London for a day or
two only, as he said, leaving me in charge.
Then, at the time fixed for his return, Mr.
Wade came in his stead. It appeared that
Mrs. Wade had suddenly decided upon a
short visit to America with the children;
that the father of the family, finding Bedford
Place dreary without it, now transferred himself to Paris for change of air and scene. He
would occupy, of course, a room in our small
apartment over the bank in the rue Saint-
Arnaud; and I despatched our man-of-all-
work, Isidore, at once, to make it ready.

This apartment which I, myself, inhab-
ited, of which nominally, too, I had the care,
was one of the joys in my Paris life. A sunny
suite, well furnished, it stretched along, *au
premier*, with no intervening *entresol*, above
the banking-rooms of the ground floor, on
two sides of a picturesque inner court, — one
of the airiest in that airy quarter, a stone's
throw from the Opéra. The small Hôtel des
Victoires, well known to English and Americans, backed into the court on the third
side. On the fourth side there were no win-

dows, but only a high wall overgrown with trellised vines.

A quaint, low building with a flat roof arranged as a terrace filled a portion of the space on the hôtel side. There lived our *concierge*, old Vincent, and his wife, Céline, who together guarded the great doors leading to the street at the end of a dark archway. A thick-leaved linden tree shaded their humble dwelling. The court was paved with flagstones; but there were flower-beds about its central fountain and along the walls. All the precincts were kept immaculate by this pair of good Parisians, who had been the caretakers, Heaven knows how long! In all sights and sounds, the place was peacefulness itself, rarely invaded even by a strange footfall; for the main door of the bank opened into a thoroughfare on the other side of the building. Here, the Hôtel des Victoires overlooked our domain, indeed, from its back windows, but had no right of entry. That belonged only to us and to the unobtrusive tenants of the apartments overhead whom we hardly knew by sight.

Paris can be very hot at the end of July,

and that summer was a normal one; yet, somehow, there the heat never became unbearable. George Wade even went so far as to declare that it was essential to his comfort. "And comfort," he would say, as we settled placidly for dinner at the open window of some *café* on the Boulevard, "is attained here, as nowhere else on earth. Look around you at these simple *bourgeois*, drinking their bocks contentedly upon the pavement. God's air is their pavilion, its canopy the stars! Then think of the stupid Saxon stuffiness of London; think of New York! This is a great people, Tim! It cuts its coat according to its cloth, and triumphs over conditions."

When the day's work was done, and on Sundays when there was no work to do, we two were natural companions, sufficient for the time unto each other. We made sundry excursive flights from our own quarter up and down the river; but often we dined at home in our pleasant *salle-à-manger*, opening upon the court. There, after dinner, putting out the lamps, we would withdraw for coffee and cigars into the high wide window, watching the ripple of the fountain, or listening

to the linden's murmurous branches in our
intervals of silence, when we were not engaged in the discussion of life's problems.
These we handled without gloves, as men
will when two are thrown together intimately;
and we two soon grew as intimate as youth
and middle age can ever be, each amused by
groping in the dark for the other's point of
view. Occasionally would come a disturbing
gleam of light from the semi-distant Hôtel
des Victoires, to make us by common instinct
lower our voices; but that occurred infre-
quently, since the season was over, and many
of the back rooms there were closed. Otherwise, no mortal ear could overhear us except
the four attached to old Vincent and his wife
in the court below; and these to English
speech were deaf as adders.

On one of those quiet evenings, *à propos*
of the linden, George Wade began unconsciously to hum, "Woodman, spare that tree!"
Then, at my request, after protesting that he
had not done such a thing for years, he proceeded to sing it,—so well, that his appre-
ciative audience of one clamored for more.
He had forgotten his words, he said; but,

presently, delighting, as I could see, in my delight, he believed that he could "render" "Oft in the stilly night," if I wanted it. This — a tremendous success — led to another of Moore's melodies. The ice was broken; he had gained confidence, and he rejoiced to find that his memory and his baritone voice alike stood by him. Nightly recitals followed as a natural consequence; he willingly "rendered" something from a source of supply that seemed inexhaustible whenever I suggested it.

They were all songs of an earlier generation, the more grateful to me on that account; unfamiliar strains, generally sad, to words of Hood and Scott and Burns as well as the melodious Moore. Scott's "Outlaw" became my favorite. It suited Wade to perfection, and was, indeed, as the foreigners say, his battle-charger. The maiden on the castle wall and her episodic lover were given due dramatic effect; while the spirit of romance seemed manifest in every note of the sweet refrain : —

> " O, Brignall banks are wild and fair,
>   And Greta woods are green,

>   And you may gather garlands there
>   Would grace a summer queen."

My own spirit it was, in all likelihood, that controlled me; for I was then at the romantic age, easily swayed by feeling, unable, if I would, to draw the line between a just proportion of sentiment and an excess of it; but that he sang the song well there can be no doubt.

By way of ending with the best, I usually begged last for " Brignall banks," as we called the song; and one dark night, when we were just about to turn in, he sang it for me. The day had been intensely hot; around us the windows stood wide open, including one or two in the hôtel, which seemed to indicate that some of its back rooms were occupied. As he reached the last stanza, I caught the gleam of a white garment in a window there opposite our own, and made a sign to draw his attention that way; but he had seen it, too, and, leaning forward, addressed his final phrase to that vague presence: —

>   " Maiden! a nameless life I lead,
>   A nameless death I'll die;
>   The fiend whose lantern lights the mead

Were better mate than I!
And when I'm with my comrades met
Beneath the greenwood bough
What once we were we all forget,
Nor think what we are now."

The words rang out with fine fervor of
expression, turning the song suddenly into
a serenade. This compliment was acknowledged by a murmur of laughter, low and
sweet, cautiously repressed; the dim figure
vanished for a moment, but presently reappeared bearing a lighted candle, which
showed the presence to be that of an extremely pretty young girl.

She was all in white, with a gold chain
about her neck and a thin line of gold on her
uplifted arm. In her dark hair a jewelled
ornament gleamed; her eyes— dark, too —
flashed in the candlelight which fell full
upon her face. She stood there long enough
to give us a good look at its youthful lines,
broken, irresistibly, as it seemed, by a winning smile, brighter than the flame; then,
with another low laugh, she blew out the
light, bent toward us in the dark to close the
shutters, and was gone.

We waited on for another song or two persuasively applied in her direction; but she would neither come back nor make a further sign. Long after bedtime we still sat up comparing notes about her. Mr. Wade insisted that she was Spanish, while I thought her an Italian; at all events, she must be of some Southern outlandish race, as we both agreed. It was arranged that one or the other of us should make researches at the hôtel the next day to decide the important question. So we parted for the night, and I soon fell asleep to dream of Haidée, Astarte, and other Byronic heroines, — all romantically distressed, but all elusive.

The next morning, before my companion was stirring, I took coffee alone and went over to the hôtel for a study of the visitors' book. With the help of the *concierge*, who showed a lively interest in my search, I marked down the quarry, — a matter of some difficulty, since the hastily scrawled indications were by no means precise. After vainly attempting to attach our fair unknown to a group of Russians, whose rooms proved to be in another part of the house, I found that the only quarters in use on our side were taken by " Dr. Keswick and party, Mobile, Alabama." An American, after all! But to make sure, I pursued inquiries a little farther. Of what did the party consist? Eh b'en, the Américain was an old monsieur, bel homme, young for his years. He had with him a jeune fille and a maid. Voilà tout! His daughter, of course; the thing was clear. I returned triumphant, to proclaim the news to George Wade, who sat in very light attire over his coffee-cup. She was Miss Keswick, of Mobile!

" I said a Southerner," he growled.

" Keswick, perhaps, is a Spanish name," I retorted.

" No; Italian!"

" I still think she is of Italian extraction," said I.

He laughed. " Let us hope, at least, that she understands English; otherwise, the songs were wasted. I think her grandmother was a Cuban, Tim!"

" We will settle the question," I answered, " as soon as I have made her acquaintance."

" Ah! you mean to do that?"

" Of course."

" Beware of the dog, then, — I mean the doctor, who is young for his years."

" Oh, he 's a trifling obstacle."

" You are very sure of your conquest, my boy. Well, good luck go with you ; only let me warn you to prepare for disappointment."

" How so ? "

" Because," said George Wade, lighting his pipe ; " because she has probably lost her heart to me already. As the girl says in ' Twelfth Night' : —

' Poor lady, she were better love a dream.' "

" A rare old charmer, you are ! " I rejoined ; " especially, in your present dress ! But there would be no conquest without rivalry. I shall try, all the same."

In spite of my assurance, I could not quite determine the first step, and made no advance that day ; frankly admitting this, when night came to find us at the window in our accustomed places. The field was his, and he took possession of it, filling the court with song, — to no purpose, for the shutters of the Hôtel des Victoires remained obstinately closed. Ten o'clock struck, reminding him of a French air which all Paris had caught from a pretty comedy — "Les Cloches du Soir" — performed nightly at the Gymnase; and he took up the refrain : —

> " Dans les prés fleuris,
> Sous les églantines,
> Allons nous asseoir, —
> Pour entendre encore
> Leurs voix argentines,
> Les cloches du soir ! "

As the notes died away, the opposite blind swung open slowly, and Miss Keswick, as now we called her, appeared at the window. She was in black this time, — more Byronic even than before, like a Queen of Night, bespangled with gold that glittered and flashed in the bright light of the room. She smiled upon us — for an instant only ; in the next, half turning as if at a step behind her, she laid her finger upon her lips with a look of dismay, and drew in the shutters. The light went out ; that glimpse was to be all.

"The watch-dog is on duty," laughed Mr. Wade. "To-night there must be no more singing. All the better ; to bed, at once ! or we shall oversleep, and lose our Sunday at Fontainebleau."

We were both up betimes to make that holiday excursion for which the morning promised well. The court, when I looked out upon it, was flooded with sunshine; with water, too, at the moment, since the indefatigable Vincent, splashing his hose about, had flushed the pavement. I glanced at the closed shutters opposite, and felt sure that something stirred behind them; consequently, in reply to the *concierge* who greeted me and remarked upon the weather, I spoke not only to him but to whomsoever else it might concern with emphatic clearness.

"Yes," I agreed, "it is a fine day. We take the 9.30 train to pass it in the country,—at Fontainebleau."

"All day!" rejoined the simple retainer, falling plump into the trap; "the gentlemen will breakfast then, probably, at the Black Eagle."

"The Black Eagle, surely. It is a very good place, as we are told."

"The best, monsieur. I can assure monsieur of that, for we were many years in its

service, my wife and I. It has the best position, the best kitchen, the best wines —"

"And the best custom, too, no doubt,"
said I, laughing; "there one may hope to
meet one's friends, eh?"

"Assuredly, monsieur. Bon voyage, et
bonne fortune!"

I thanked him, with a weather-eye, as it
were, on the Hôtel des Victoires. From the
shuttered window a white veil flashed out, as
if by accident. I produced my handkerchief
and flourished it with an affectation of carelessness. The veil flickered in response, but
was instantly withdrawn when George Wade
joined me.

He laughed derisively upon hearing of my
pointed conversation.

"Do you hope to find Miss Keswick in
the train?" he asked.

"Stranger things have happened," I returned. "All the world goes to Fontainebleau. Why not a Southern sight-seer with
the rest?"

"You are a very sanguine adventurer," he
declared.

I was altogether too sanguine, as the

events of the day proved. Nowhere at either
station was there any sign of her. In the corridors of the château, in the green crossways
of the forest, I searched for her persistently,
but ever in vain; until my grave companion
grew uproarious over what he called the far-
away look in my eyes.

Faint with hunger we turned about noon
into the comfortable Black Eagle, choos-
ing for our repast a table in the courtyard
under an arbor shaded by a rampant sweet-
briar.

"'Allons nous asseoir sous les églantines!'"
murmured George Wade, as he sank into his
place.

"Ah! an idea!" shouted I for joy.

"Lucky lad! What is it?" he inquired.

But I refused to tell him that until our
meal was ended, when I begged the *garçon*
to cut me a handful of blossoms from the
clambering vine.

"For Heaven's sake, why?" Mr. Wade
demanded; "are n't there flowers enough in
the Madeleine Market?"

"This is my idea!" I rejoined; "in remembrance of your song and to continue

my *conversation à trois* of the morning. A harbinger of friendship for Miss Keswick!"

"Here's devotion! Henceforth, I am mute and leave you in possession of the field. It is useless, I suppose, to refer again to the watchdog."

"Quite; for I am bitten already; and, besides, these are dog-roses, — that's their other name, I believe."

"I see, — sops to Cerberus. Well, Lord help you and your floral tributes. Go in and win, Tim, — if you really want her."

Somehow, that last remark acted upon my spirits like a douche of cold water. I had used the word friendship advisedly, meaning no more than by a small attention to carry on our harmless jest. Here was Benedick, the married man, already taking it seriously. The thought that she might do the same made me a bit uneasy. Then, I reflected that she, herself, had taken the first step forward, — and I dismissed the qualm. Surely, she must understand that my move to meet her was a part of the joke. We were playing with sparks, not fire.

In the return train I wrote on one of my cards : —

For Miss Keswick
Les églantines de Fontainebleau

— leaving flowers and message with the *concierge* of the hôtel, as we passed its door.

We dined at home, and from my seat at table I glanced frequently through the open window toward the hôtel, hoping for a glimpse of her. The twilight drew on without that pleasing apparition; it was already dusk when the opposite blind swung out, and I saw her at the window, holding up my " floral tribute." She perceived and acknowledged with a smile my gesture of gratification; then, leaning forward, she flung with all her strength a white object toward me, and instantly was gone again. The projectile flew no farther than the terraced roof of Vincent's quarters, where it gleamed, rebounding and settling down at last, conspicuous as a snowball. I hurried from the table, through the service corridor to a side window, out upon the terrace and back again, before George Wade had recovered from the shock of my abrupt flight. Then, chuckling, I displayed my trophy, which proved to be a letter wrapped around the coin of the country — a *gros sou*. He, having seen and understood nothing, inquired what that white thing was.

"A message — by balloon post!" I replied, airily; "so important, that I know you will forgive me for reading it immediately." And, without awaiting his responsive growl, I tore it open.

This was the letter :—

Your flowers are *too lovely!* But what a mercy that the *concierge* handed them to me and not to Grandpa Keswick! My name is quite different, you see — but how could you know? Ma is his daughter — we left her in Mobile, and I am travelling with him alone. Your songs are *sweet*, — I just love them and wish I could stay at home and hear them all to-night, — but we are dining with Mrs. Morgan Hitch, of Augusta, Georgia, who lives in the loveliest place, up near the Arc. Do you know her? She is a *dear* — and has promised to bring me to the bank some morning to see you. You must not speak of it to *any one* and must be *surprised* when you see me. PLEASE be *very careful!* Grandpa K. is an AWFUL BEAR!!

> Yours very truly,
> NORA PENRHYN.

P. S. Isn't it all strange—and romantic? I feel as if I had known you always.

While I read and re-read these potent words which were written, according to current fashion, in an angular character of enormous size, George Wade went on with his dinner, and a prolonged silence fell between us. I saw, of course, that he waited for me to speak, and I deliberately kept him waiting. It was he who spoke at last, moved by ungovernable curiosity,—in a tone which betrayed some displeasure at my reticence.

"Well, how is Miss Keswick?" he demanded, gruffly.

"There isn't any," I declared, laughing, and pocketing the letter with a grand air of discretion.

"What do you mean? Explain yourself!"

Thereupon, I gave him her name. There could be no harm in that, since he must learn it, sooner or later; nor in establishing her true relationship to her travelling-companion; nor in a casual mention of her friend, Mrs. Morgan Hitch; nor, finally, in Miss Penrhyn's odd mistake in attributing his songs to me,—a mistake which seemed to afford him much amusement. Sooner, rather than later, he thus learned the greater part of her message, and was mollified.

"So she has turned into a—what do you call it?" said he;—"a Penguin."

"Penrhyn!" I corrected.

"I can never remember that," he protested; "the other is easier. I shall always call her the Penguin."

"Her name does n't matter, after all," I argued. "She will soon change it. Tell me what you know of Mrs. Morgan Hitch, who seems to have established hers. Did you ever hear of her?"

"Hitch! Hitch?"

"*Morgan* Hitch!"

"There used to be such a name on our books. I know I 've seen her,—a slender, faded woman in black, I should say, one of the Paris-American colonial horde."

"That is she, of course. Will you introduce me to her, when she comes in?"

"Oh, she's coming in, is she?"

And he was master of all Miss Penrhyn's message now.

During the next few days, the message was followed up by a shower of white missiles that dropped like falling stars into our court, — messages joyous and messages despairing, — now to tell me that I might expect a visit at the bank upon the morrow, and again sorrowfully to contradict the news; to console me with a knot of crimson ribbon or an ornament in filigree, apparently meant to be worn in the hair. Upon Miss Penrhyn's discovery that her eyrie overlooked my desk in the bank as well as the dining-room table, the missives came thick and fast, — so often that I longed for an air-gun to transmit more readily my acknowledgments. Always there was a note of apprehension in them. "Grandpa" was on the alert; or her maid, Dinah, whose complexion I discovered to be of the *café-au-lait* variety, had "suspicions."

Dire results — unspecified — would surely follow, should our dreadful intrigue be detected;
and when a black scarf waved at her window, on no account must I present myself at
my own. She was like some Eastern princess
in a tower, watched and guarded by malevolent spirits, while my unswerving devotion from afar was always assumed and emphasized.

I packed away the tokens, and sent, by
favor of the *concierge*, enigmatic lines addressed to her in a hand properly disguised,
— did my best, in short, to intensify the romance in which it seemed as if she hardly
dared to draw breath. This, however, was no
easy matter; soon, indeed, I confronted the
inexorable law of change in all human relations of the earth, — the insecure grasp upon
the pleasant glow of the passing moment,
which is dissipated in the next, never to be
recovered. So long as our opposite neighbor's
identity remained a mystery, — when she
might have been a titled heroine with an inexplicable past and a problematic future, —
George Wade took in her the keenest interest. The edge of it had dulled perceptibly

when through my investigation she turned
into an American summer tourist; and now
that, fully identified, she was merely Miss
Penrhyn, of Mobile, Ala., — he dwelt derisively upon the official abbreviation of our
Gulf State, — there was no edge left. He
would not even raise his voice for her benefit; discontinued our song - recitals; made
reference to the late transactions, as he called
them, only in the most sarcastic vein, speaking of her always as the Penguin; until I
chafed under the weight of his cynical indifference, finding such a confidant worse
than none at all.

I have sometimes thought that, all the
while, he was really interested to the point
of anxiety, persisting in his idle comment as
a kind of cold-water cure, which he deemed
expedient, if not essential to my welfare. But
of this I have no proof. I can only say that
he sustained the assumption, if it was one,
mercilessly and invariably.

So stood the case, when, one morning,
the bank-door opened, admitting two veiled
women, richly dressed, in the younger and
more timid of whom I recognized Miss

Nora Penrhyn. She stood in the background smiling tremulously, while her chaperon came to the front, and announced herself as Mrs. Morgan Hitch. There was nothing timid about her; nor was she the slender, faded woman in black of George Wade's haphazard recollection; on the contrary, her figure, voice, and bearing were alike floridly redundant.

"I think it possible there may be letters for me," she explained; "will you kindly send and ascertain? Mrs. Hitch, — Mrs. Morgan Hitch, of Augusta, Georgia! Mr. Garner, I believe! This is my friend, Miss Penrhyn."

I bowed with becoming gravity as to strangers of distinction, begging them to be seated, while I sent a junior clerk in search of the letters, nonexistent though I knew them to be.

Mrs. Hitch merged herself in the leather sofa cushions, and became at once a warmly intimate friend.

"What delightful rooms!" she declared. "You just love it, don't you, here!" She pronounced the last word "yere," and I soon observed that the not unpleasing ellipsis and prolongations of the negro dialect pervaded all her speech. "This is the quarter I adore, — the *Dame aux Camellias* quarter, I call it, — she lived in the rue Louis-le-Grand, you know, round the corner. But when we settled, Mr. Hitch stood for the Arc, so it had to be! It's Paris, all the same, 'de Batignolles à Romainville,' as the song says. You love every stone of it, don't you, Mr. Garner? Yes, I know you do!"

I listened, laughed, and watched Miss Penrhyn's eyes twinkle mischievously behind her veil, until my messenger came back with the report that there were no letters. At the same moment George Wade appeared to evoke my silent blessing; for of him Mrs. Morgan Hitch took immediate possession. They had found common acquaintances to discuss in an instant; in the next they were chatting like old friends.

"At last! after all these days!" whispered Miss Penrhyn, though the others were deep in their talk, and no one else could overhear us. "I'm right glad! Isn't it strange — exciting? You are not so old as I expected, and—" Here she hesitated, blushed and gave a thin, nervous laugh which I soon found to be habitual.

"And you are younger than I thought," said I; whereat she laughed again; "less beautiful, too!" I might have added, perceiving at a glance, that candlelight and twilight across the intervening court had been all to her advantage. The veil she now wore was a thinner one than these afforded; and the face behind it seemed sallow and expressionless, unformed, childlike as the figure; for she could hardly have been more than seventeen. Even her eyes, though large, dark and lustrous, were too prominent for perfect beauty. The laugh, *à propos* of nothing, suggested lightness if not vacancy. It was unquestionably a shock to find in my Haidée and Astarte of the Parisian summer night only a giggling schoolgirl.

Meanwhile, happily unconscious of these cruel reflections, she went on in her confidential whisper : "I was dying to come, you know, but Mrs. Hitch could n't bring me till now. She 's ever so nice, plotting and planning for us. We 'll meet often now, won't we?"

"I shall give myself the pleasure of call-

ing upon you at the Hôtel des Victoires,"
was my awkward reply, the quality of which
I seemed unable to make a shade less chilling. The shortcoming passed unnoticed.
"Oh, no, no! on no account!" Miss Penrhyn hastily protested, clasping her hands,
as if in agony at the thought. "You must
never come there,— never! Grandpa Keswick
is awful! Victoria,— Mrs. Hitch will arrange
it. Trust to her!"

Before I could ask why such excess of
precaution was necessary for a visit presumably formal in its character, Mr. Wade was
handed a telegram, and, excusing himself,
drew apart to read it; while Mrs. Hitch,
breaking in upon us, forestalled me.

"Oh, Mr. Garner," she urged, breathlessly;
"I wanted to ask you to dine with me on
Thursday — most informal — just ourselves
— me and Nora, with one or two others —
Wally Wicketts, perhaps; you know Wally?
No? Well, you 'll love him, won't he, Nora?
Say you 'll come!" Here, Miss Penrhyn's
hand touched my arm with a gentle pressure,
and I had accepted before I was well aware
of it. "That's right, Thursday at eight—

forty-three, avenue de Jena,—forty-three! Nora, darling, time's going; we shall be late at Estelle's! Good-morning, Mr. Wade, — so pleasant to have seen you! My purse? Oh, yes; how reckless of me! Now we're really off! Good-morning! *Good*-morning!"

I ushered them to the door for an effusive parting on her side, on Miss Penrhyn's an impassioned one. We two clasped hands tenderly, and she waved me from the lower step a fond farewell. Then I turned back to find George Wade convulsed with laughter.

"That's a breezy lady!" he chuckled; "but I congratulate you upon your Penguin. She's a monstrous pretty bird!"

"'My Penguin'! You take my breath away,—and so does she. I dine with her on Thursday, *chez* Mrs. Morgan Hitch!"

"I envy you. You will have the dinner of your life."

"Tell me, if you can," said I,—"you must know all about her now. Who is Mrs. Morgan Hitch?"

"Oh, yes; now I have oriented her. She is not at all the person I supposed."

"So I inferred. Who, then, is she?"

"The Southern wife of a Northerner, — a Pennsylvanian, I believe, who is immensely rich. He made a fortune in steel, — or was it *steal?* At any rate, there is some kind of a cloud over him. He finds it convenient to live abroad."

"She wears her cloud lightly."

"My boy, it has a golden lining. She was of the poor and proud order, — a noble Georgian, without a dollar to her name, until she accepted his and its attendant millions. She wallows now in wealth, more or less ill-gotten, bearing her hard fate like a true Parisian, — or, rather, like an out-and-outer of our American colony, which includes, roughly speaking, a thousand of the same sort. There is no harm in her otherwise, I imagine. It will amuse you to see her establishment, — once. Go, and eat off cloth-of-gold; I want to hear about it. You won't have to swallow him, for they agree in disagreeing. As the poet says: Wife dines at Edmonton, and he at Ware!"

I made a wry face, and shrugged my shoulders. At that expression of distaste, George Wade laughed the more.

"Don't be fastidious! This is a phase of life which you have never seen. Exile washed with gilt! And you may spell that last word with a '*u*,' if you please. Embrace the opportunity! Go it, while you're young! It's your privilege, Tim, — your duty. Only, — look out!!"

"One other question; answer me, if you can. Who is Wally Wicketts?"

"Ah, there you have the advantage of me. I never heard of him."

All this occurred nearly forty years ago, and, in consequence, I retain but a confused impression of my dinner at forty-three, avenue de Jena, though it was, in respect to inordinate luxury, as my mentor foretold, the dinner of my life. Briefly summed up, it might be called a festival of surfeit. The splendor of the decorations, lights, service, food, displayed on all sides wanton excess. We must have been twelve at table; but most of the company I had never seen before and never saw again; their names and even their faces are gone forever. I sat on the left of my hostess, who looked as if she had overeaten all her life and was oppressed

by the weight of her jewels. She seemed to
delight in tender references to her husband;
yet he was not present, his place being more
than filled by a noisy Silenus from Milwau-
kee, too stout for all his garments. Opposite
me sat a pale young man, silent, arrogant
of manner, who was presented for my benefit
as Mr. Walter Wicketts, of Mobile. According to Mrs. Hitch's word, in a subsequent aside to me, he was "extremely good
padding"; yet he contributed little to the
hilarity of the night. Thin and colorless he
came, thin and colorless he remained, not-
withstanding a relishing appetite and his
own remarks thereupon, which stamped him
alike as *gourmand* and *gourmet*. The padding,
judiciously bestowed within, did not obtrude
itself.

Among these companions, Miss Penrhyn,
in her Queen of Night bespangled garb,
shone like a star. Promptly I retracted my
critical judgment upon her looks, agreeing
with George Wade that she was "monstrous
pretty," — almost with Mrs. Hitch's charac-
terization of her as "a dream of loveliness."
She sat afar off upon the opposite side of the

table, but one remove from the boisterous winebibber ; and across the intervening lights and garlands she established at once with me a signal-code which was maintained through many courses of the dinner.

"Nora uses her eyes so well, the dear ! " whispered Mrs. Hitch, with belated consciousness of these proceedings; "and she adores you, Mr. Garner ! If it should n't come off, what a crying shame that would be ! Mind, now, whatever happens, I 'll stand by you ! "

This last phrase set me wondering to what I stood committed that should need her proffered support. I remembered George Wade's injunction to "look out," and, after that, looked out another way, during the rest of the dinner, neither receiving nor despatching signals. The pursuit of an innocent pastime, undertaken as a lark, otherwise meaningless to me, seemed to others dangerously significant. Though Mrs. Hitch applied her flattery with a trowel, I felt myself puffing up under the application like a pouter-pigeon. If Miss Penrhyn meant anything at all, the time had come to cry quits, and call it off.

How should I conceive that it would have been impossible, perhaps, at the moment to choose a better method than mine of bringing it on?

The men smoked outside upon a terrace overlooking a walled garden, bright with flowers. There, under the stars, we grouped ourselves about Mr. Hitch's substitute, the swollen Nestor of the feast. Lured on by "Wally" Wicketts, who became odious to me, the garrulous old pagan led the conversation into a monologue. He told tales of adventure, audacious, yet so amusing as almost to justify themselves. I had seen his type before, and have encountered it often since, but can remember no one who approached him in the art of scandalous narration. This exhilarating episode of half an hour might have continued until daybreak, if the hostess had not recalled us. As we obeyed her summons, she took possession of Mr. Wicketts, assigning me to a seat beside Miss Penrhyn. Near by was the open door of a conservatory, into which presently we moved; there for the next few minutes being left to ourselves.

She began with questions of my life in Paris, in which she professed to take the strongest interest. Until then, I had hardly heard her voice, and was struck at once by its soft Southern cadences, its unaffected gentleness. The laughter annoyed me less than at our former interview; indeed, after the first few moments, I ceased to think of it, for she was in a quiet, deferential mood, leading me on to talk, content, as it appeared, to listen, listening well. My critical faculties were lulled asleep; charmed by this new aspect of her, off my guard, I listened to myself a little, as, at times, we all do. While I proceeded, she grew grave, intent; she hung upon my words. I paused, and there was a silence. Then she asked: —

"And are you to live here always?"

"I hardly know. At least, I hope so."

Smiling at the thought, she sighed, too, and said: —

"It all sounds so delightful! I envy you; I would give the world to live in Paris."

At that moment from the drawing-room came a rollicking piano prelude, whereat she stirred impatiently. The air, thrice fa-

miliar, was a favorite of the hour in the
London music-halls; immediately a man's
voice took it up.

She made a wry face, and laughed discord-
antly.

"It's only Wally Wicketts," she whispered;
"we need n't go in yet."

I settled back in my place, prepared at
her bidding to ignore both song and singer.
Then followed the refrain, which there was
no ignoring.

"If ever I cease to love!
If ever I cease to love!!
May the income-tax be a shilling in the pound,
If ever I cease to love!!!"—

rang out to the delirious joy of the company;
and, this time, it was I who laughed.

With a look of comic despair Miss Penrhyn
rose instantly and led the way toward the
drawing-room.

"No use!" she declared; "we can't talk
now; but come here any day, after five,—
you 're sure to find me."

Turning to say this, she ran into the arms
of Mrs. Hitch, who had crossed the threshold in search of us.

"Oh, Nora, darling!" gasped the genial obstacle. "Don't be the death of me! So here you are, sly creatures! Come along, Mr. Garner; I want to hear you sing."

"Sing!" I repeated. "Sing? I am sorry, — but that's quite impossible."

"Nonsense! Come!"

"I assure you that I do not sing a note. I have never even tried."

Mrs. Hitch stared, first at me, then at Miss Penrhyn, in blank amazement.

"What!" she cried; "but, Nora, dear, I thought—"

Miss Penrhyn, with heightened color, only laughed by way of answer.

"I see!" interjected I; "it's all a mistake. It was the other one you wanted. You should have asked Mr. Wade, instead of me."

This, however, Mrs. Hitch, regaining composure, instantly denied.

"Not at all!" she declared. "We wanted you, and no one else. Did n't we, Nora?" Then, at a burst of applause behind her, she went on, turning back into the room: "That's splendid, Wally, boy! Don't stir from that piano! Give us your whole repertoire! Keep straight on!"

And on he kept.

I had no further confidential words with any one, that night, until the moment of leave-taking, when, as I shook hands with Miss Penrhyn, she whispered: —

"After five, here. Remember!"

She swept down the staircase to her carriage on the arm of Mr. Wicketts; and I found myself hearkening to the same reminder, echoed by the hostess in her most cordial tones: —

"I am at home always after five, — and not at all in anybody's way, — ha! ha! you understand! Good-night, Mr. Garner. So very nice of you to come. *Good*-night!"

Murmuring feeble words of compliance, I, too, passed down the stairs and out amid the wide, deserted vistas of the fashionable quarter, which the Arch of Triumph and Rude's heroic sculptures glorify at all times and seasons. The homeward trail of the Champs Élysées blazed on before me in long lines of gleaming lamps; slowly, thoughtfully I took it up, to follow it, pondering.

The evening's adventures, amusing as they were, gave me in revision an unpleasant sense of entanglement. I laughed at them, yet laughed uneasily. The joke had been a good one of its kind, but it had gone far enough. I was tired of the meshes of implication, which at every contact with them seemed to be more tightly drawn ; I must extricate myself at once, then and there. But how to do this with dignity, courteously, gracefully ? In the watches of that night I hit, at last, upon a very simple way.

To George Wade, who was keenly eager the next day to hear about "the dinner of my life," I gave what I deemed essential details with apparent frankness, confiding to him, however, neither my distrust nor the resolve which I had formed in consequence of it. I feel sure, now, that he was perfectly aware of the one, and that he strongly suspected the other; and I marvel the more at the discreet course he pursued in respect to both, never hinting at his knowledge or his suspicion, yet by methods of indirection sustaining me with good counsel and sympathy.

We dined together at a quiet, *bourgeois*

place, unaffected by the transient foreigner,
far up the boulevard. He had received a letter from his wife, and I attributed to this
the fact that he was in a reminiscent, tender
mood. He talked of married life and of home
ties — the only ones worth strengthening.
I had heard similar views from him before,
but he did not often enlarge upon them, and
I encouraged him to go on, never guessing
that, now, all this was aimed at me. Then,
as if yielding unawares to my intelligent interest, he grew more confidential, and unfolded an adventure of his early life, which,
as he said, had come within an ace of wrecking
him. On the eve of a *mésalliance*, that could
only have resulted miserably, he had awakened, as if by a miracle, to the peril of his
momentary fascination, and thus had escaped
one of the worst misfortunes possible to man.
Marriage might well be called a horrid risk,
but marriage in one's own circle he considered to be the safest warrant for the love of
a lifetime. That Italian proverb about choos-
ing wives and oxen in your native province
was as wise a saw as any ever uttered.

I listened with patient approval of his

shrewd philosophy. Then, the next day, about three in the afternoon, I called at the avenue de Jena, and sent up my card to Mrs. Morgan Hitch. She was not at home, as I had foreseen. This was my obvious method of acknowledging her hospitality and at the same time of evading the tryst which had been forced upon me, with whatever complications might ensue. I chuckled at the success of my diplomatic stroke. My duty was done; we were quits; they must understand the finality of that move, and accept its full significance.

Not so. A day or two later the Hôtel des Victoires opened fire again in a white missile from Miss Penrhyn. She wrote overwhelmed with despair at losing the pleasure of our promised interview; it was too sad that I had mistaken the time, and had come too early; but dear Mrs. Hitch now agreed to take her this very afternoon at five to Tortoni's; I must come there at that hour; it was *most important;* she implored me not to fail.

Clearly my best course, in view of all the circumstances, was to stay away. I wrote a note of formal regret, pleading an engagement; then I tore it up. To send that would involve me in further correspondence; on the other hand, absence with no word would savor of brutality. Hovering between the horns of this small dilemma, I was seized with insatiable curiosity. What did she want with me of importance so urgent? What mysterious game were these two women playing? The shortest way to learn that was to meet them half-way by keeping the appointment. To be circumspect, on my guard, committing myself to nothing, seemed an easy matter in that public place. I would unravel the skein, once for all, yet avoid its tangled web. To join in their game, open-eyed, to see what they did and how they did it, would surely make entertainment for an idle hour.

My silence, therefore, was that of acquiescence. In due season, at the carnival-hour of the day, — *l'heure d'absinthe,* — reflecting as I crossed the Chaussée d'Antin that the street of the world had never looked gayer than on that brilliant afternoon, I strolled up the left-hand side of the Boulevard des Italiens toward the Café Tortoni. That famous rendezvous is now no more; but then

it still flourished, strong in half a century's
notoriety, at the corner of its side street, with
the tarnished decorations and worn furniture
of 1830, like a page from Balzac. All stood
open to the sunshine, that day; the place was
thronged; but as I went up the steps, I caught
sight instantly of the two who sought me
there. They sat in a front window, conspicuous by the fashion of their garments,— leading the fashion, rather than following it, —
and, as they hailed me joyfully, all eyes for
the moment turned our way. "Ah! Améri-
caines!" some one remarked with scornful
inflection. The word passed, and all interest
in us with it; by that, our eccentricities were
discounted, explained, condoned; we were
lost in the crowd.

Mrs. Hitch, making room at the table,
immediately ordered for me an *Amer Picon*.
Miss Penrhyn, prettily flushed with excitement, smiled and said little; but her chaperon said a great deal, with no hint of re-
proach for my former defection; on the contrary, she was intensely, abnormally cordial.
While I listened, in bewilderment, to her infinite deal of nothing, the speaker suddenly

broke off with a despairing cry, and started up.

"Oh, my dear! I've gone and forgotten it, — the most important thing! I must have left it across the way at Christofle's. I'll run right over and be back in two minutes!"

Before we had time to question or to detain her, the incoherent Mrs. Hitch shot off, out of the café and down the Boulevard.

I understood in a flash. The game, as conducted by the arch-conspirator, involved leaving her *protégée* and myself alone together. Reckoning without my hostess, I had never thought of that. The move was made; we two were to all intents and purposes apart in the Desert of Sahara; and, caught in the snare, I could only swallow my vexation, since, whatever its just extent, escape was cut off; the utter impossibility of forsaking the girl in the front window of the Café Tortoni forcibly presented itself to me.

She saw the change in my face, and was quick at interpretation.

"Oh, please!" she entreated. "It's all my fault; Victoria won't be gone long, and I wanted so much to see you, — to ask your advice. Don't be angry! You are angry, are n't you?"

Her voice trembled; her eyes filled with tears, at sight of which my annoyance took a turn toward pity, as I answered: —

"No; I am not angry. It was something very important, then; pray tell me what it is. I will help you, if I can."

"Well, we are leaving Paris in a very few days, you see. I have just heard that grandpa has taken passage from Liverpool on the 29th."

"And you wish to stay abroad? Is that the trouble?"

"That's half. The other half is worse. It 's Wally Wicketts. He wants me to marry him. They all want me to, — grandpa, ma, and all the rest. I half promised that I would — and now — "

"You are engaged to Mr. Wicketts?"

"No, it was n't an engagement; I would n't have it so. I only said 'perhaps'; but that was long ago — oh, months! — before we came over. I did n't know, — he might have been the one — how could I be sure? but since then — "

"You have changed your mind? You don't care for him enough?"

" No, he is not the one — it is n't Wally; yet they all insist — "

"What of that? It is you who must insist. You are not bound to them. Even had you given your word and did not love him, a bad promise is better broken than kept. You would do wrong to marry him."

The color came and went in her face; supporting it upon her clasped hands, she leaned forward over the table and looked at me intently.

" You think so? You say so?" she asked.

" Of course. What right have you to marry any man, unless you are sure—sure beyond all question — that he is for you the only one on earth?"

"Sure, — sure beyond all question?" she repeated; " how can I, how can any one be really sure?"

"To ask that is to dispose of Mr. Wicketts. He is not the ideal you have imagined, evidently. We all have such ideals, I suppose; when you find yours, you will know it without advice, without argument."

" Yes, I suppose we have them, all of us,"
she agreed, laughing nervously, with averted
eyes; "and you have yours, then! What is
yours like?"

"Oh, that does not matter," I returned,
lightly. " I can only say I have never found
mine yet."

She laughed again. "I can tell you what
she's like," she declared, with sudden em-
phasis; "I reckon I know exactly. She is
blonde, petite, exquisite, delicate, graceful,
Parisian. She wears pale blue and pink roses,
—like that Nattier portrait at Versailles, —
the one with the garland; only modern as
can be, and—"

"Stop! Stop!" I interrupted, to protest
against every detail of this unfinished picture.
" All that is absolutely wrong! Do you think
I am expatriated? Mine, if she ever comes
into existence, will be, above all things, of
my own country, my own race—of my own
circle, too!" I continued, quoting George
Wade without acknowledgment. "She will
have the simplest tastes and care for the best
things there at home. I don't know about
her looks, I can't describe them; but I do

know that she will be good, kind, intelligent, lovable, and will wear what clothes she pleases—as unlike Nattier as all this here is unlike New England!"

A smile flickered upon Miss Penrhyn's lips, as her look followed across the crowded café my sweeping, inclusive gesture. "Yes, I was wrong," she admitted, in a low, quiet voice; "how should I know? I have never seen New England." She paused for a moment; then added, still more faintly: "It can't be much like this! Yet I was right, too, after all, in a way. Whether she ever comes into existence or not, you have imagined your ideal! I do certainly hope—"

Her voice broke; she struggled to control it, stopped, and once more looked out beyond me upon the noisy company. Tears glistened in her eyes. She impatiently brushed them aside, and dropping her hand to the table drummed upon it with her fingers in a painful effort to counterfeit light-hearted ease.

"What have I said?" I asked. "I did not mean—I am very sorry—" and, bending toward her, I laid my hand gently upon hers.

"Don't!" she cried sharply, drawing away the hand and still avoiding my look. Then, suddenly her whole expression changed. Colorless, distraught, she sprang to her feet with a stifled word of alarm.

I turned, and saw, making toward us between the tables, a man no longer young, white-haired but erect, with bristling mustache and cheeks flushed with rage. I did not need to be told his name. Before she could speak it, he was upon us, addressing her in an angry tone of authority.

"Nora! What's this? What, in God's name, are you doing here?"

The color returned to her face. Forcing a laugh, she went incoherently through the form of introduction.

"Grandpa! This is Mr. Garner—my grandfather, Dr. Keswick, of Mobile—"

I had risen, and turned toward him; but he acknowledged my presence only by a curt nod, without so much as a glance in my direction.

"Come!" he said, savagely, taking another step toward her and offering his arm; "come with me!"

She turned her back upon him, speaking now with perfect self-possession. "I am very much obliged to you, Mr. Garner, for your advice. I certainly am! Good-bye!" and held out her hand.

"Good-bye!" I answered; "and the best of all good wishes!"

So we shook hands, and parted. Dropping into my chair again, I watched her move slowly out on the old man's arm. At the door she looked back, caught my eye, and smiled.

I waited on alone for a while, to muse upon the situation. Then, remembering that Mrs. Hitch might reappear at any moment, I hurried off to avoid that possible interview. Whether the chaperon resumed her office or not, I never knew.

Often, in the following week, I looked across our tranquil court, beyond the linden-tree, at the Hôtel des Victoires, for some chance glimpse of Miss Penrhyn, but none was afforded me. Perversely, I now regretted this. Having chafed under entanglement, I actually caught myself longing for its meshes. The longing, however, was intermittent and easily conquered. "She will write before she sails," I thought; yet no letter came.

I remembered the date of her departure, and, when it had passed, sought her name in the Liverpool passenger-lists. There, booked for New York, I found in due course : "Dr. Keswick, Miss Nora Penrhyn." It was late afternoon; we sat at our desks, signing letters; I leaned back in my chair to look up at the hôtel-window. Astarte had vanished, —there would be no Haidée any more!

George Wade, idle at his post, must have divined my thought, for his voice rang out in the quiet office with startling aptitude.

"By the way, Tim," he asked, "what has become of the Penguin?"

"Ask of the winds!" I laughed in answer, tossing him the newspaper. "She has spread her wings, and flown from us across the weltering sea."

Chuckling, he looked down the column at the names. "*Tant mieux pour tous!*" he muttered; and sank into silence behind his desk again.

They were playing "Frou-Frou" at the

Gymnase, that autumn, with the incomparable Desclée in the title-part. The tragicomedy, since become a minor classic, is enrolled now in the repertoire of the Comédie Française; but then its fame was new; the world, high and low, flocking to see it, overran the small theatre of the Boulevard. Late in the winter I saw it, too, and was immediately struck by a strong resemblance in the frivolous heroine to Miss Nora Penrhyn. She had gone out of my life; for months I had not thought of her; yet as I walked home, that night, by the Café Tortoni, her vivid presence went with me. "Yes," I thought, glancing at the window where we had sat together, "that is her type, — a Frou-Frou of Mobile! What has happened to her, I wonder? What will happen? What will be her end? Some day, perhaps, I shall hear and know."

That day came at last, though it was far removed. The momentary impression faded to an idle memory, lingering unheeded in its abandoned brain-cell, rarely recalled. More than fifteen years had passed, when an accident revived it. A chance acquaintance, who had once known her, casually spoke her name. My curious inquiry led to identification, — then to the complete story.

She had yielded to insistence, and had married Wally Wicketts; the short term of married life with him proved most unhappy. She had ended it abruptly by desertion, eloping with a lover, who, in his turn, deserted her. Friendless, far from home, she had fallen ill, to die alone, miserably, in a public hospital; and she had been dead for years.

That was all — a sharper tragedy than the French dramatic parallel, which some prophetic sense in me found applicable! Long and persistently I was haunted by its dreadful ending. To the last day of the Café Tortoni, I could never pass it without seeing her face in the window. Other fifteen years are dead and gone since then, twice over; yet, even now, I stir sometimes at the phantom recollection, and taking up my cue again, like the hero of the Gymnase murmur to myself, aside: " *Frou-Frou! Pauvre Frou-Frou!* "

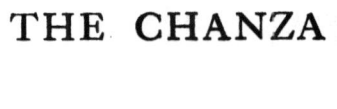

THE CHANZA

THE CHANZA

WHEN Dr. Graham Frankland, the distinguished anatomist, began his short address before the Scientist Club on that December evening, none of the hundred members present could have foreseen the inexplicable and uncanny nature of his subject. The club, as its name implies, is composed chiefly of grave and reverend savants, though it includes from other walks of life a few hardheaded, practical men who are of an age to take things seriously, — at least before supper-time. For it is a recreative club, so to speak, meeting once a month only at the house of some hospitable member, for mental refreshment first, — in the illustration of a new scientific discovery, or of an old one newly applied, — and physical refreshment afterward. Its sixty years of life attest the wisdom of its founders in thus convoking the assemblage with a double purpose, upon the express condition that both forms of incentive should always be of such excellence as to whet the appetite. And the original high standard has been so well maintained that to-day membership becomes an enviable honor, while regular attendance is instinctive.

Before this intelligent and animated company of his *confrères* Dr. Frankland plunged abruptly into Amazonian wilds, to recount the traditional custom of a fierce Indian tribe, said to have existed there for many hundred years. According to his statement, it was their barbarous practice to decapitate hostile chiefs slain in battle, afterward subjecting the heads to an unknown process which, preserving the features intact, reduced them to the size of a small apple, without shrivelling or even wrinkling the skin in the least. The process, whatever its character, must have been a rapid one ; for nine days after the victory the head, thus dwarfed but not defaced, was set upon a pole at a sacrificial rite, there to be harangued and insulted by the slayer. Another chief, detailed, as it were, for defence, impersonated the victim, making the bitterest retort to each abusive word. At the end of this curious dialogue the head was taken down, the mouth was sewed up,

that it might never speak again, and the grim
trophy became an object of reverence, wor-
shipped, thereafter, as an idol. Removal of
it was a grave misfortune; since, if it were
stolen and passed from hand to hand, the
worst of luck inevitably attended its possessor.
A head so treated, degraded, and revered was
called a " chanza."

This was the pith of Dr. Frankland's interesting if somewhat improbable tale. After
unfolding it in general terms, he supplied certain details, by way of confirmation. Declar-
ing that several specimens of the chanza in
the past had been transmitted to civilized
countries as curios by missionaries and otherwise, he displayed photographs of two such
examples still existent in a foreign museum.
While these were handed about among the
audience for close inspection, the anatomist
prepared his final *coup*. From a silken bag he
suddenly drew forth his own specimen, lately
acquired, — a head, conforming in every
particular to his description, perfectly pre-
served in little, with thick black hair a foot
and a half in length.

A ripple of excitement spread through the

room. The doctor's well-calculated dramatic surprise had been entirely successful. Smiling, he went on to say that at first sight, believing the head to be a clever fraud, a mere image with no real relation to life, he had tested it in more ways than one. The microscope soon showed conclusively that the hair was not inserted, but had actually grown from the scalp. He had proceeded, next, to dissection. The orifice of the neck was closed by a mass of dark, resinous substance, hardened by time. Upon removing this he found a scrap of white paper lined with blue, which proved to be the piece of a modern envelope. Upon this were scrawled indecipherable hieroglyphics. Below was stuffed a lump of soft cotton, in which lay entangled fragments of safety-matches. These seemed, at first, to be splints, supporting the nose; but further examination disproved that theory. The doctor decided that the bits of wood had been caught up accidentally in the cotton, which was pronounced by an expert to be Peruvian, of rare quality. To reconcile these proofs of civilization with the ancient custom had then become the investigator's task. The Indian chiefs now living admit the performance of such a sacrifice centuries ago, but assert that it has ceased to exist. The tribe, however, is a large and scattered one; and the doctor believed that the rite still holds — in remote sections, at least. In his opinion, the head was a genuine chanza, but modern, a trophy set up within twenty years.

In conclusion, Dr. Frankland speculated briefly upon the mysterious reducing process. The skull, of course, was removed at once; after an incision, the skin was carefully turned back and as carefully replaced. Certain missionaries have supposed that the head was then boiled for a time with native astringent herbs, or that it was filled with hot stones and ashes. He, himself, conceived that the two methods might have been employed successively. But all that was pure conjecture. The only certain, tangible thing was the head, which each man present could now examine at pleasure. And amid general applause he passed it to the veteran president of the club, who sat beside him.

" Very well done! " whispered one of the audience in a remote corner of the room to his nearest neighbor; "I should not have expected that from Frankland."

The speaker was George Matlock, the noted novelist, a keen, restless, dark-eyed bachelor of fifty, in whose nature things went by contraries. His attitude toward the world was that of a thorough skeptic, shrewd, adroit, incisive ; when the door of his library closed upon him, he became a dreamer, blessed with a vivid imagination, a subtle fancy, and a tender heart. His vein of originality, though not vast, had never been overworked. He had won fame's rewards early, and still they showed no signs of waning, thanks, so some of his envious rivals murmured, to his less estimable qualities — to what they called the business end of him. For, despite his success, perhaps in part because of it, he was not loved among his fellows.

Philip Armistead, in whom Matlock had confided, was a man under thirty, not yet enrolled in the club membership, but invited by the host as a guest of the evening only. He held the clerkship of a government office, devoting his spare hours to small excursions into the field of fiction. These had met with so much critical success as to warrant his hope that he might, some day, make literature his sole pursuit. In the mean time, athirst, as it were, in a dry place, he dwelt upon the hope feverishly, neglecting no opportunity that seemed likely to advance its fulfilment. He studied the aim and drift of contemporary masters in his chosen art, longing to breathe the same atmosphere, to assimilate their methods and habits of thought. The Scientist Club, which he now saw for the first time in session, interested him profoundly, as well as significantly; his very presence among these men of renown being a forward step in his ambition.

Of Matlock, whom he already knew, Armistead had the disciple's awe, the disciple's envy. Matlock stood securely where he desired to stand. Moreover, the man of success had stooped from his height to bestow upon the beginner an encouraging word, for which he still felt grateful. It was natural, therefore, in this strange company, that he should first seek Matlock out, and that, a moment later, he should accept the vacant chair offered him next Matlock's own. Sitting there, he had watched the proceedings intently, and had been particularly impressed by the queer story of the chanza, with no suggestion of that possible double-dealing on Frankland's part which Matlock by his whispered word implied.

"You don't believe it, then," Armistead responded.

"Do you?" asked the other, shrugging his shoulders.

"I neither believe nor disbelieve," said Armistead. "If Dr. Frankland —"

"Bah!" Matlock interrupted, carelessly; "an ingenious hoax — no more. We shall force Frankland to confess it; you'll see."

They relapsed into silence, while the object of their comment, passing from one hand to another, came slowly toward them. Matlock followed it closely with his eyes, a circumstance which Armistead, who had swiftly engendered an idea of using the chanza as material for a story, noted in a kind of jealous pang. The eager look, so much at variance with the expressed indifference, forced upon him a suspicion that the master, struck by the same thought of the chanza's

literary possibilities, had mentally appropri-
ated it, and was now trying to throw him off
the scent. The suspicion, once formed, grew
apace, and as they waited on, still silent, he
studied Matlock with catlike intensity, that
no sign of proof or disproof might escape
him.

At last the man in front turned with a
smile and gave the head to Matlock. He held
it lightly in one hand and tapped it with the
knuckles of the other — for an instant only.
Then, superbly apathetic, he held it out to
Armistead.

"There you are!" said he.

As Armistead's fingers closed upon the
grewsome relic a sudden chill shot through
them, not from the thing itself, which felt
like parchment and looked like darkened
terra-cotta, but from an immediate conviction that these fine, handsome features, diminutive as they were, had once been flesh
and blood; that life had once indued with
sight the half-closed eyes. In the next moment he felt as if some spark of life still remained there, as if the thin lips might move
and speak were he to cut the thread that

bound them. He turned the head, and the touch of the long hair upon his hand induced a shudder. Another moment passed, in which all this repugnance gave way unaccountably to fascination. He would gladly now have taken time for scrutiny of the minutest sort. But the man next him stirred impatiently, and just then upon his shoulder came a warning pressure. He glanced down, and saw there a strong, dark hand, wearing a ring of strange design, its beaten gold and enamel shaped into the device of a harpy-like figure—a bird with a human head. Mechanically he passed the chanza on to his expectant neighbor, and turned to see who had given him the signal. Behind stood a group of men, one of whom drew back, avoiding Armistead's look; and his was the only unfamiliar face.

Armistead plucked Matlock by the sleeve. "Who is the tall, dark man standing here behind us?" he asked.

"Which one? Oh, Dallas, you mean,—Dallas, the Latin professor."

Dallas, indeed, was one of the group. Armistead, however, knew his face well enough, and this he was about to say; but the stranger had moved away out of sight, making further inquiry futile at the moment; so he merely murmured a word of thanks for the superfluous information.

"Well, what do you think of the chanza now?" Matlock demanded, sportively.

"That there is probably nothing in it," replied Armistead, obeying an instinctive impulse to conceal the peculiar spell that its nothingness had wrought upon him.

Then came a general displacement of the audience in quick response to a hospitable word from the supper-room. Armistead rose and slipped off into the crowd, disregarding Matlock's laugh of satisfaction, which would surely have confirmed his own suspicious forecast of the novelist's purpose to make the chanza profitable. But Armistead no longer concerned himself with that. He was intent now upon finding the stranger whose hand had touched him so insistently as clearly to convey some warning or command. He had caught a mere glimpse of the man's face, but would identify it, of course. Even the hand — a left one, with the grotesque ornament upon its third finger — he could not fail to recognize. He hurried from room to room, brushing by acquaintances or nodding to them abstractedly, engrossed in a vain search. That strange face was nowhere to be seen. Before long an intimate friend, clutching his arm, called him to account for his eccentric behavior. Thus admonished, he came to himself, and, following his mentor to the supper-table, clinked glasses with him in token of sanity, then withdrew to make a second round of the rooms, on his guard now, counterfeiting composure.

Near the speaker's table several club members clustered about Frankland, plying him with questions concerning the chanza, which had returned to his keeping. Armistead, joining them, listened to this cross-examination that strengthened in all particulars the direct testimony. The doctor stood his ground stoutly, in manifest good faith. One by one the others dropped off, until Armistead, left alone with the anatomist, begged permission to take the head into his own hands again. Once more he held it, once more its deadly chill benumbed his fingers, yielding, as before, to an attraction that was irresistible. While Frankland, noting intelligent sympathy, discoursed upon the finer points of his subject, Armistead felt convinced that some third person behind him had drawn near to listen. Yet when he turned there was no one within ear-shot. Startled, he let the head fall, but by good fortune it dropped only into the silken bag, which at that moment Frankland held out to receive it. Both the start and the resultant bit of awkwardness thus passed unnoticed.

"I see that my trophy interests you," remarked the doctor, with a smile.

"Immensely!" said Armistead, masking embarrassment with enthusiasm.

"For further data inquire at my laboratory," continued Frankland, drawing the strings of the bag together. "I have all the documentary evidence, which I shall be glad to show you there at any time."

"Thanks; I will come. May I ask how long the chanza has been in your possession?"

"A very short time. I have but just secured it. A week ago to-morrow it was — to be exact."

" Ah ! And — and — " Armistead hesitated for a moment, then went on. "And nothing has happened ?"

" Happened ? " repeated the scientist, wrinkling his brows.

Armistead laughed, as if to prove that his speech was not to be taken seriously. " Nothing unpleasant, I mean," he explained ; " you said that, according to local tradition, removal of the idol foreshadowed grave calamity. Has it brought you no ill luck ? "

" None yet," laughed the doctor, " in spite of the legend. Since its discovery the relic has been owned by three men before me. Each in his turn, as I am told, in a fit of nervousness, became most eager to dispose of it. But, thus far, I have no such tremors. We may hold, perhaps, that science has the power to nullify even the most occult of ancient charms. Come, let us drink together and avert the omen ! "

In the supper-room they encountered Matlock, whose spirit of chaff seemed now ungovernable. The full force of it he launched at Frankland, who, admitting nothing, denying nothing, answered him in kind with im-

perturbable good humor. Armistead, leaving
them to their fencing-bout, again sought in
one room and another the stranger whose
shadowy intervention had so perplexed him.
But not even so much as a shadow of the
unknown could anywhere be discerned. A
movement of departure had already set in.
Armistead fell into line with it, shook his
host's hand, and strode home alone the shortest way, meeting no one, for the hour was late,
the clear winter's night intensely cold.

Armistead's solitary walk had been haunted
by a vague apprehension, which even the familiar aspect of his lodging at first did not
dispel. He turned up lights, flung open cup-
board doors and peered into dusty corners,
half prepared to challenge a possible intruder. But all was undisturbed. His comfortable bachelor quarters overlooked a city
park at the corner of two thoroughfares.
The streets, so busy by day, were now deserted, silent. Beyond, black shadows of the
elm trees in a long vista lay motionless upon
the frozen earth. He drew his curtains, and,
stirring his fire, sat down before it. In its
cheerful glow the evening's events, the club

meeting, the talk, the chanza, the strange attendant presence already began to assume the illusive likeness of a dream. And as one records a dream's impression in the moment of awakening, lest something of value should escape beyond recall, Armistead was moved to make, then and there, in black and white, notes of the night's adventures. Taking pencil and paper, he hurriedly set down a summary of Frankland's discourse for future use. But when he tried to supplement this with a description of the chanza, connected thought seemed suddenly to fail him. He nodded, yawned, nodded again, and dozed, then dropped into sleep, and slept profoundly.

He woke with a start at the jar of a closing door below—the street door, as the sound informed him. It was past three o'clock; the fire had died down; his hands were numb and cold. But he sat still a moment longer, listening to a man's step that came heavily up the stairs. Slowly it reached his landing, stopped there for an instant which chilled him with absurd fear of an untimely visitation. Then the step passed on

to the floor above. A door opened, closed
again, and all was quiet, except for an intermittent, muffled footfall overhead. He sprang
to his feet, recovering from the momentary
alarm that had been groundless and unreason-
able. This was merely some fellow lodger
returning home belated. He did not know
the lodger, as it happened, so much as by sight,
and now could not even remember his name.
But the step treading lightly back and forth
along the upper floor had the quality of com-
panionship. It was no longer a disturbance.
He went to bed, to sleep, and it affected him
not at all.

Waking late the next morning, Armistead
dressed in a hurry, then rang for his breakfast, which, as usual, was brought to him by
the man-of-all-work, a garrulous old Frenchman of the watch-dog type. The man had
once been a soldier, and now devoted himself to this alien service with well-disciplined
fidelity. Armistead detained him for a moment to ask a question.

"Jacques, who lives upon the floor above
me?"

"There, monsieur?" demanded Jacques,

in a tone of surprise, with an upward jerk of the thumb.

"There, — yes; just overhead."

"No one, monsieur. Does not monsieur remember?"

"But they are not vacant still."

"Si fait, monsieur. For the moment, yes. They are rented again, as I am informed, but the new tenant has not yet arrived."

"He has arrived. I heard him last night."

Jacques raised his eyebrows incredulously. "At what hour, monsieur?"

"He came in late, very late. At three o'clock it was."

"There is some mistake. The rooms are still unoccupied. I think that monsieur was dreaming."

"Nonsense! I sat here wide awake, — here by the fire, — and heard his step distinctly."

Jacques shook his head. "But the apartment is quite empty — the door not even locked. Monsieur can assure himself if he will go up and see."

They went, accordingly, together, finding the door unlocked — within, mere emptiness over which light streamed through the open shutters. Waiting at the threshold, they looked in upon the bare floors thickly over-laid with dust. This bore nowhere the trace of any footprints; yet when they trod upon it their own steps immediately were made visible.

"Monsieur sees truly that it was all a dream," said Jacques, with a triumphant smile.

"I am forced to believe so," Armistead admitted. "And yet I could have sworn — "

"Spare the oath, monsieur; it would be wasted. We are only men. Such things, at night, may happen to any man alive."

There was cheer in that simple philosophy which Armistead soon persuaded himself to accept unreservedly. Overcome with sleep at the fireside, he must have slept on, dreaming so vividly as to fancy himself awake. During the next few days nothing occurred to change this rational conclusion. The rooms above his remained unoccupied and silent, so far as he knew. Meanwhile, official matters of importance left him no leisure for work at home, where his hastily written notes upon the chanza were thrust aside — neither neglected nor abandoned, but awaiting better opportunity.

When at last the freer hour came, Armistead's first thought was to take a long, meditative walk in the twilight, according to his habit of stimulating thus the inventive faculties. Intent only upon this open-air solution, as he called it, he followed unfrequented streets, absorbed in his new theme of the chanza, considering always how best to turn it to account. He had brought his notes with him, and with their help, over a simple dinner in an obscure foreign restaurant, he hit upon a plan which pleased him so well that he determined to work it out at once. On his way home the plan developed in his mind, assuming definite shape, ready to clothe itself in words. He had now but to hold the pen and guide it. The night lay all before him; more than that, since the following day was Sunday, at least thirty-six hours of liberty were to be his. He would use them to good purpose.

The sky was overcast; already light snow-flakes filled the air and swirled up along the

pavement. Armistead pressed on toward his
projected task, but at the familiar street corner he stopped suddenly, for he saw with
surprise that the windows above his own
were lighted. Through their half-closed shutters a steady glow, as if from a lamp, streamed
out upon the gathering storm. The new tenant had arrived, then! Yet, after all, what
should startle him in that, since the arrival
had been expected daily? Armistead's second
thought dismissed the trivial circumstance.
Passing up into his own rooms, he settled
himself at the writing-table and plunged deep
in work — so deep as to pursue it long with
scarce a break. The occasional sounds from
the street were deadened by the new-fallen
snow; indoors, all was tranquillity itself.
Now and then, at first, he listened for some
movement overhead. But nothing stirred
there. Either the new neighbor was most
peacefully disposed, or he had gone out, leaving his light behind him. In either case,
Armistead blessed him for the great gift of
silence, and soon ceased to consider its possible cause.

He wrote on for several hours in a continuous flow of thought, which was checked by an obstacle proceeding from the work itself. His notes were defective in important details of the chanza which he tried in vain to supply from recollection. It was just here that memory had failed him before on the very night of the meeting, and the subsequent lapse of time confused his impressions hopelessly. The more he labored the more bewildering they became. Dropping the pen, he reviewed his work. All had gone wonderfully, and much had been accomplished. The hour was late; it would be best, perhaps, to stop then and there for the night. In the morning he could call upon Frankland for another look at his treasured curio, and make accurate notes of it on the spot. Had not the anatomist signified his readiness to permit this at any time? Decidedly, that was his best course. After all, he had no reason to be dissatisfied with his progress. In beginning well he had bettered expectation.

So he caught up the loose sheets of manuscript to arrange them in their proper order, when a sound stayed his hand—the sound of a heavy step upon the stairs. He had heard

that step before; and now, as he listened to
it, trembling with a nameless fear, his heart
beat wildly. Once more it drew nearer,
reached his door, to waver there for one ap-
palling moment; then went slowly onward.
Again the nocturnal visitation was not for him.

But now Armistead let fall his papers,
sprang to the door, opened it cautiously, and
looked out. A gas-jet burned there in the
hall to guide late-comers; and by its light
he saw a man's figure moving up the staircase. He took a step forward, and waited,
with eyes fixed upon the next landing, where
the stairs turned at a right angle to the upper floor. There the man looked down, and
the light shone full upon his face; his look
met Armistead's; he smiled faintly, then
passed on out of sight. But Armistead had
recognized at once his fine, dark features. It
was the stranger who had touched his shoulder at the club meeting, and either by chance
or by design had afterward eluded his search.

This, then, was the lodger overhead!
Armistead, in blank amazement, shrank back
into his own quarters, closed his door noise-
lessly, and listened. Silence, profound silence;

no step, however faint, could now be heard.
What manner of man was this who came and
went, as if by occult means, leaving no trace
behind? Wild curiosity tempted him to follow the stranger up and demand an interview.
But on what ground could he do this? How
at this hour call to account an inoffensive
lodger, without some reasonable excuse? The
man had established rights that must be respected. No; he would go to bed, to sleep,
and leave investigation, direct or indirect,
until the morning. Jacques, the watchful
Jacques, could enlighten him in all probabil-
ity with a single word.

He tossed restlessly the whole night
through, without a wink of sleep, straining
his ears for sounds that never came. The
lodger overhead gave not the smallest sign
of life. The first gray light of morning
soothed his tired senses, and he slept at last,
peacefully, for several hours. When he woke
again, refreshed, in a normal state of mind,
the sunshine streamed into his chamber, and
it was almost noon-day. He summoned
Jacques at once, ordered breakfast, and then
said with an air of light indifference: —

"So our new lodger has turned up, eh?"

"Oh, yes, monsieur, he moved in yesterday."

"Ah! indeed, and who is he? Is it some one whom I know,—who will be a good neighbor?"

"Undoubtedly, monsieur. At least he knows monsieur by name; he said so."

"So much the better. What's *his* name, then?"

"It is,—ah! 'Cré nom! I have it at my tongue's end."

"What! You have not forgotten it?"

"Si, monsieur; but that's no matter. I have his card; I will bring it with the coffee."

"Do so, by all means."

When the card came he doubted his own eyesight. The name upon it was "George Matlock."

"Impossible!" he cried. "There is some mistake."

"No, monsieur, none whatever. That is the card—the gentleman himself gave it to me. Monsieur does know him, then?"

"Yes, but—it is incredible! He has taken the rooms, you say?"

"Yes, monsieur, and furnished them, —
well, too, as monsieur will see when he
calls."

" Yes, yes, I shall call immediately. Is he
there at this moment?"

" No, monsieur. He has already gone out
— for the day, as he said. But he will return
to-night. Monsieur may, surely, see him
then."

"Good!" said Armistead, handing back
the card. "Then I shall surely see him. I
had not heard of his coming; it surprised
me."

"But monsieur has no fault to find with
his neighbor?"

"On the contrary, he is more than welcome."

"Ah! So much the better for us all!" rejoined Jacques, cheerily; and wishing Armistead a good appetite, he shuffled away.

Left alone, Armistead settled down into
composure. The news, though unexpected,
could not be called disquieting. If it failed
to account for the stranger's presence in
the dead of night, that was Matlock's affair,
admitting probably of some simple explana-

tion, should Matlock choose to give it. That again was Matlock's affair, not his. When they met he would touch lightly upon his own relations with the stranger, and for the rest be guided by inspiration of the moment. To proceed diplomatically, avoiding direct questions, would be wisest.

He had the afternoon before him for his own affairs. His first care was to read thoroughly his work of the night before, bringing daylight and the invaluable fresh eye of the thoughtful craftsman to bear upon it. Though the changes were few, time slipped by in considering them. It was already late when, confronted with his old difficulty of doing full justice to the chanza, he put away the manuscript, and, taking a note-book with him, started for Frankland's house. To his disappointment the anatomist was not at home. But the servant believed that he might be found at his laboratory in another quarter of the town. And thither Armistead hurried on.

The old building, used as a dissecting-room by Frankland's grandfather, the foremost surgeon of his day, stood in a retired street otherwise given over to stables and store-houses. Their black, unlighted windows seemed to frown dismally upon Armistead in the dusk. From one roof, however, halfway along the street, a skylight gleamed. That was an earnest of welcome. The light came, as he knew, from the laboratory, where Frankland must now be at work.

The outer door was closed, but not locked. Armistead pushed on in the dark, up one rickety staircase, then another, to the top of the building. Light shone there from an inner door, half open. He knocked; but getting no answer, stepped in.

The room was long and narrow, heightened by the gabled skylight in the middle of its dingy ceiling. On either side stood glass cases filled with rare specimens, strange instruments, models in wax yellowed by time — grim relics of surgical triumphs, long forgotten. On a shelf above the cases stood a row of plaster casts — masks of the living and the dead, with dusty labels. Over one of these, at the old operating-table, which now held only musty pamphlets, bent Frankland, scrutinizing the face closely.

He started at Armistead's step, with a look of vague alarm, almost of terror, which he tried hastily to shake off. But his features, white and worn, seemed old unaccountably. In spite of his welcoming smile he was ill at ease.

" Armistead! " he cried. " Glad to see you! Sit down — here, if you like! "

Armistead hesitated. " I am not in your way, I hope."

" Sit down! " he repeated, heartily ; then in another tone he asked: " Did you meet anybody on the stairs ? "

" No one," said Armistead, wondering at the question. As Frankland made no comment, after a pause he resumed : " You asked me to come, and I have taken you at your word."

" I remember," said Frankland, gravely ; " to see the chanza. But to-day you are too late, my boy — an hour too late."

" Too late ? "

" Yes ; because another fellow has stolen a march upon you. He shared your curiosity — came to-day to see the head, and I let him carry it off."

"You have lent it to him?"

"Indefinitely. I told him to keep it as long as he pleased. I am tired of the thing."

"Ah! And — and the documents?" stammered Armistead, taken aback by the disconcerting news.

"The documents are here," returned Frankland, putting down the plaster cast and stirring the heap of papers upon the table; "some of them, at least. See! This is a letter from the Amazon missionary who first unearthed the chanza; this, the voucher from our consul at Pará; and here is a tracing of the hieroglyphics discovered by me inside the trophy. The original I replaced."

He smoothed out the transparent sheet, displaying the cabalistic signs inked upon it. Armistead started. Among them he recognized instantly the harpy-like figure of a bird with a human head — the device of the ring that once had pressed his shoulder upon the third finger of the stranger's hand.

"I see!" he murmured, and stared at the tracing with startled eyes. There could be no mistake. In form, in size, the two symbols were identical.

"A curious, grotesque language," pursued Frankland, unaware of Armistead's agitation; "possibly archaic — inscrutable, at all events. If one had the key, now, to decipher and interpret it! But for that one must look to Mundrucù Land."

"To Mundrucù Land?" Armistead repeated.

"Yes. The Mundrucù Indians, far up the Amazon, are the inventors of the chanza, — a peculiar type, fierce, barbaric, it may be, yet not without intelligence."

"You know the type, then."

The anatomist nodded, and pointed at the rows of casts lining the upper walls. "That is the collection of the once famous Spurzheim, exponent of phrenology, — the pseudo-science, whose principles we now dispute. But something of value lurked within it, and that remains. At Spurzheim's death my grandfather bought the contents of his workshop for a song, and here we have them. I found, by accident, this very day, the life-cast of a Mundrucù. Let me have the honor of presenting him to you!"

He turned back to the cast upon the

table with a bantering air which struck
Armistead as forced, unnatural. And as he
lifted the heavy bust his hands trembled.
" There," he continued, striving to be calm ;
" that is the type."

Armistead rose, drew nearer, then drew
back, clutching his chair for support. Speech
failed him. The features of the life-cast bore
a resemblance, close, unmistakable, to those of
the mysterious stranger whom he had last seen
at midnight on the staircase of his lodgings.

For a moment the two looked at each
other in silence, with drawn faces, white as
the cast itself. Then Frankland spoke.

" You have seen him, too ! " he whispered.
"When ? Where ? "

Armistead drew a long breath. Frankland's
words, amazing as they were, brought with
them unspeakable relief. They proved beyond
a doubt that the recurrent presence was no
creation of his own disordered imagination,
but, at worst, a living man of whom the scientist possessed some knowledge. Recovering
himself, he hastened to answer Frankland's
questions, to question in his turn. The mutual
confidence was an encouragement to both.

It appeared that Frankland had first encountered the stranger in the street, by night, on his way home from the club meeting. Since then the man had hovered about him persistently for some purpose which could only be surmised. That very afternoon here, in the laboratory, he had heard a heavy step upon the stairs; and, going to the door, he had recognized his tormentor, who, at sight of him, turned and sped away, out into the open air. Noting the likeness to the Indian cast, he had taken it down; and was convinced that the features, if not the same, showed the same distinctive qualities. Then, for the first time, he had connected the haunting presence with the chanza — an object of peculiar veneration to those who contrived it. And he now believed that the stranger was neither a spy nor a common thief, but a cunning, devout fanatic, charged with an important mission; namely, the recovery of the sacred relic and its restoration to his tribe. Merely this, no more; a human being, not a supernatural agent. In our day and generation that was inconceivable.

"In which case," continued Frankland,

with a reassuring chuckle, "you and I have seen the last of him. The chanza is out of our keeping. Heaven be praised! Its responsibilities rest with Matlock now."

"With Matlock?" echoed Armistead, in astonishment.

"Yes; what did I tell you? I have lent the infernal thing to Matlock, to keep as long as he pleases."

"To Matlock?" Armistead reiterated.

"Yes, once again. What is the matter with you?"

Then Armistead hurriedly imparted his old suspicion that Matlock secretly desired to make use of the chanza for story-telling purposes — a suspicion strengthened by the fact that it was actually at this moment in his hands.

"Matlock is there now at work, of course, — in the rooms over mine!" he cried angrily, provoked, in spite of himself, to jealous irritation.

"What! He lives over you?"

"Yes; he has just taken the rooms."

"Go home, then, and put him on his guard, at once."

"Why should I? He will scoff at me."

"Then we will see him together. He must be warned. Who knows to what length this savage Indian may go? By fair means or foul, he will have the chanza!"

"Very good. Matlock may listen to you, if not to me."

"Off with you, and wait for me in your lodgings. I'll follow you there as soon as possible. If Matlock is at home, go up; that's better. I will join you."

Armistead obeyed him with all possible despatch. Turning his corner, he looked up, to find that Matlock's windows were unlighted. And since the novelist had not returned, he awaited Frankland's coming in his own rooms, pacing them to and fro for a whole hour; then another. All was quiet, within and without. Yet impatience made him feverish. The minutes dragged on; and still Frankland did not come.

At last the door slammed below. He went out, looked down, and saw the scientist taking the stairs at a bound. He met him upon the landing, and drew him in without speaking.

"Sorry to be late!" explained Frankland,

gasping for breath. "Professional visit! That detained me. Why did you not go up to Matlock? I hoped to find you with him."

"He has not yet come in."

"But there is a light in his rooms."

"What! Impossible; I have heard no sound."

"I am sure of it. He must be there at this moment."

They turned to go, but stopped, breathless. A sharp cry rang through the house. There was a scuffle overhead, a heavy fall that shook the ceiling; then a groan and silence.

Together they rushed out and up to Matlock's door, which was unlocked; and, flinging it open, they went in.

The room was richly furnished, but littered with torn papers. Scraps of manuscript covered the rug, the hearth, choking the embers in the fireplace. A lighted lamp stood upon the table, and in its glow they saw Matlock upon the floor, just where he had fallen. His knees were drawn up, as if convulsively, his face was horribly distorted.

Frankland bent over him. "The man is dead!" he whispered.

"Look there!" Armistead whispered back.

He pointed at the table, where lay a sheet of paper on which had been scrawled a cabalistic sign, — the harpy-like figure of a bird with a human head. There, too, lay tattered shreds of the silken bag that had once contained the chanza. But the chanza itself was gone.

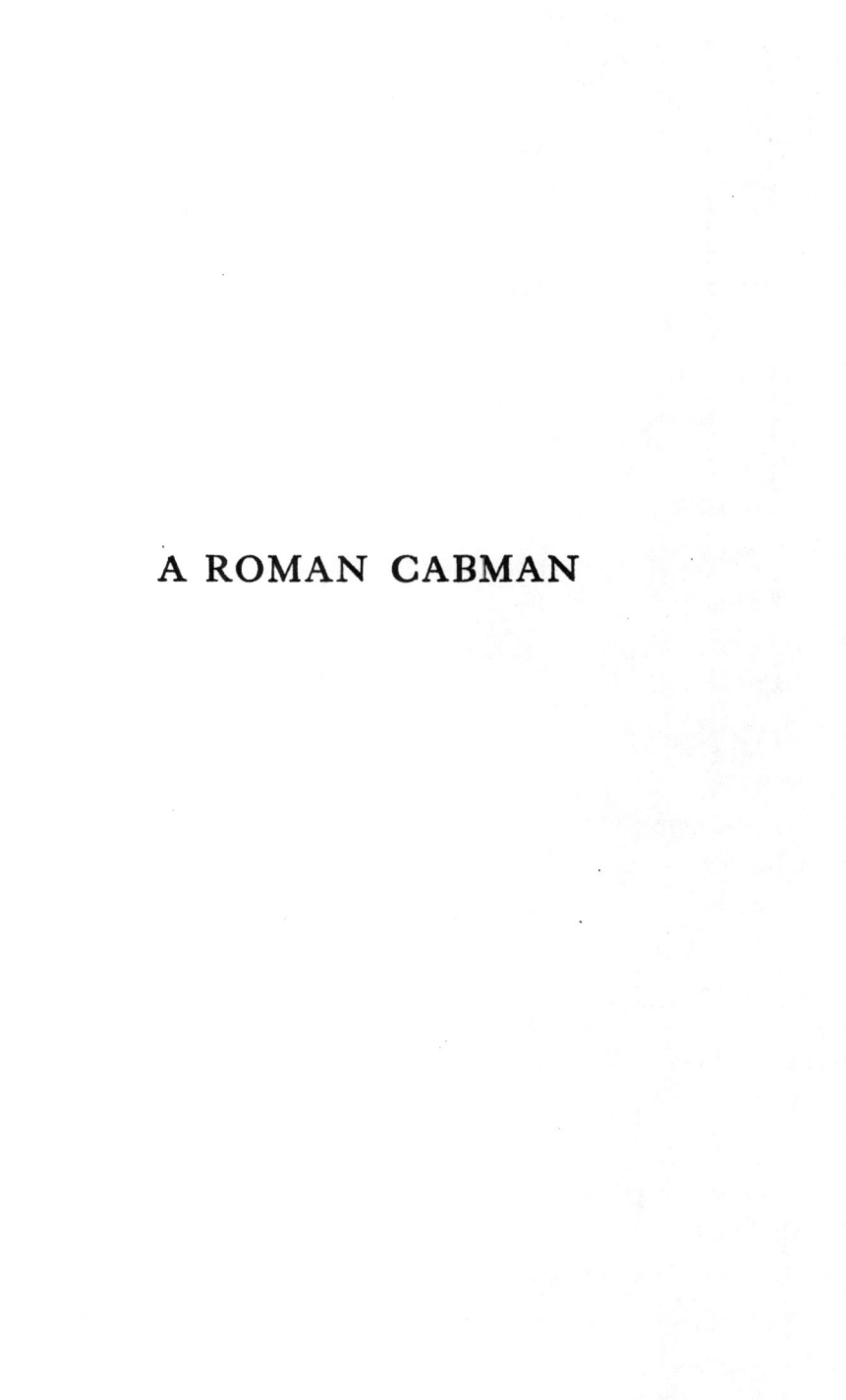

A ROMAN CABMAN

A ROMAN CABMAN

IT was in the vast, solemn precincts behind St. Peter's that I saw him first.
Coming out under the pale November sky
after a morning in the Vatican sculpture gal-
lery, I suddenly found the cabstand at its por-
tal the most grateful sight in Rome. He
stood third or fourth in the line, and he had
neither moved nor spoken, though his eye
caught mine with a sympathetic sparkle. I
saw that his small, black horse was plump
and glossy, that the whole equipage, from
his own dress to the well-brushed cushions of
the open victoria, looked scrupulously neat;
and, bidding the man drive to the Piazza di
Spagna, I sprang in, with no thought beyond
that of making this last course in a busy
morning as comfortable as circumstance
permitted.

"Your horse wastes no time," I said,
when we came out into the great square, and
shot across it through the spray of the fountains towards the bridge of Sant' Angelo.

"No, signore; the Moor is never lazy.
That is his name — the Moor, from the accident of his color, as one sees; he eats well,
sleeps well, and goes on all his four feet —
not so badly."

"And is treated not so badly — as one
also sees."

The man laughed. "Eh, signore, we have
nothing to complain of, either of us. We
understand each other, the Moor and I, and
take the world lightly."

"'A merry heart goes all the day!'"
thought I, with Autolycus. "What better
motto for a cabman?" Then, thinking aloud,
I added, "You are a very cheerful philosopher."

He turned to look down at me, laughing
louder than before. "I am a man, like another. *Che, che!* After fifty years of life, one
adjusts himself to the seat — or *Dio mio!* one
gets down, signore!"

There was no more to be said, just then,
for we had crossed the river, and our intri-
cate way toward the Corso deeply engaged
both the Moor and his master. Meanwhile,
their cheery vigilance impressed me so favor-

ably, that when I spoke again it was to secure them for the afternoon; and by the
hearty wish for good appetite given me as I
alighted at the hotel door, I was convinced
that the master, at least, if not the Moor,
still found cheer in the prospect.

I sat, smoking, near a window that overlooked the courtyard, when the man drove
in at the appointed hour. And, waiting on
to finish my cigar, I had for the first time a
good look at him. In figure he was below
the middle height, broad-shouldered, sturdy,
and erect; naturally dark, he was bronzed
by years of Roman sunshine; his cheeks
were deeply furrowed, his features large and
clumsy, plain indisputably; so that his face
would have been heavy, dull even, but for the
smile that seemed always to lurk under his
gray mustache, and the responsive light in his
sharp, black eyes. The soul of good-humored
jollity illuminated him now, as he stood chatting with the *portier;* the horse put up his
nose for a caress, and he turned in his talk to
stroke his Moorship's neck affectionately.
The hint thus given of their pleasant com-
radeship suggested a familiar horse-dealing

phrase, which, mentally, I applied to both. "Sound and kind!" I thought; and found no occasion to qualify that first judgment through any after knowledge. In all my travels along the world's highways a sounder and kinder pair than this, most assuredly, I have never known.

That afternoon, we drove far out upon the Campagna, where my tired brain sought rest and rumination from the morning's labors. The sky had clouded over, and in the mild, gray light the softened plain, stretching hazily off to the Alban Hills, brought to eyes over-occupied with artistic detail their natural refreshment. We followed the old Via Latina, at first, toward the arches of the Claudian Aqueduct, by grass-grown walls and crumbling tombs; then, turning from the straight road, we took a winding cart-path, through open meadows and rough pasture-land, into the heart of the wilderness; until, nearer than Rome itself, stood out the white villages of the snow-capped hills, — Genzano, Ariccia, Rocca di Papa, — my companion identified them, one and all, — and the wine of Genzano was not so bad! At a sharp turn of the road we drew up on a bit of rising ground, to consider the strange, sombre landscape; and, looking back upon the city walls and towers, I asked my genial guide where he lived. Pointing with his whip, he explained that he lodged in the Trastevere, close under the Janiculan Hill; as we looked, in line with the cathedral dome. Then I inquired his name, and learned that he was called Bianchi Andrea — the surname coming first, in the usual Italian fashion. And when I commented upon this custom, "Why not?" said he, "since every one calls me Bianchi — except my wife." Ah, he was married, then? "Oh, yes, signore." And he had children? "No, signore; there was a child once — a daughter — but, alas! . . . there is a grandchild, signore — a boy, who lives with me — very quick and capable — Hector is his name."

We drove on, encountering no living creature but a shaggy dog, left on guard over his herd that grazed in a neighboring field. An inquisitive pair of crows circled lazily above our heads; then, with croaks of disapproval, flew off to join their flock hovering over the great sepulchral tower on the Appian Way.

Between us and that noted landmark of the
Campagna stood a solitary farmhouse to which
my *vetturino* drew attention. One could find
fresh eggs there at a bargain; we must pass its
door; might he have the signore's permission to buy the raw material for an omelet, to
celebrate his name-day, which fell upon the
morrow? To wait for a little moment only?

Of course this favor was granted him; and
as we approached the farm I looked at it curiously. Never had I seen a drearier dwelling-
place. The stucco of its walls was stained and
weather-beaten; the outbuildings were ruin-
ous; all seemed deserted as well as neglected,
for no one stirred to question us. A whistle
from Bianchi was unanswered. "Agostino!"
he called; then, muttering, "The boy sleeps,
lazy hound!" he handed me the reins, with
a "Permesso, signore?" and went off upon
his errand.

The haze was fast turning into mist,
through which I heard the sound of wheels.
It came from a peasant's cart, rude and cum-
bersome, with the customary wisp of hay attached to a forked stick projecting from one
of the shafts. At this primitive lure, just out

of his reach, the horse, as he labored toward
me, made ineffectual plunges. I watched his
slow advance with a smile, suddenly discovering that I was watched in my turn by the man
and woman who sat behind him. They wore
peasant costume; the man, gray, uncouth, list-
less, held the reins loosely, as if he were half
asleep; but his lack-lustre eyes fixed themselves upon me with a vacant look, strangely
forbidding. The woman at his side, though
by no means old, had faded early, after the
manner of her countrywomen. Yet her face
showed signs of former beauty; and she had
in her bright colors an air of self-conscious
picturesqueness that suggested a posing *con-
tadina* from the Spanish Steps, rather than a
toiling one. As if she fancied that my smile
was meant for her, she leaned forward to return it, and seemed about to speak a friendly
word. But either her intent changed, or I de-
ceived myself; for she drew back without the
greeting, and to my good-day only muttered
a forced reply. "He is a foreigner," I heard
her say to her companion as they passed.
Then at a little distance, both turned to stare
again intently; I looked away; looked back,

to find them still staring. So they moved out of sight mysteriously, like spectres of the mist, leaving a chill behind them.

The sinister effect, however, was only of the moment. In the next, out came Bianchi, with the farmhand whom he had called Agostino, — a shy, sickly boy, who turned from me with a smile to wish his compatriot a merry night of feasting. At this word, Bianchi pointed to his small purchase of eggs, wrapped in a red handkerchief. "Ecco, signore! Per la festa di Sant' Andrea!" Chuckling, he stowed them carefully away under the box-seat, and we drove off; slowly, at first, for the road was heavy and steep. As we climbed up from the hollow, the sun burst through the clouds, glorifying the ruined farm buildings, when I turned for a last look at them, with a shaft of golden light. But now before the door, where I had waited, stood the cart which had passed me by; two peasant figures, descending from it, entered the house; they were gone in a flash; yet, clearly enough, they were the figures that I had seen — the man and woman whom my presence for some reason had disconcerted.

The sunlight faded, the mist shut down. Consultation with Bianchi shed no gleam upon my small adventure. He had not seen the uncouth wayfarers, nor could he recognize them by my description. The farm was leased to a shepherd, who acted as agent, or *fattore*; honest, as men went, — we were none of us saints, nowadays; he was absent in the pastures, as the boy had stated; if one chaffered well, having the wit to invent a "combination" and to make the most of it, he sold his eggs at a fair price. Perhaps the stranger had come to drive a bargain; they, too, perhaps, kept the feast of Sant' Andrea! Why not?

We drove back to Rome in the twilight; and long before reaching the city gate I had dismissed the intruders from my mind. But to dismiss is one thing, to forget is another. Who shall say that the brain really loses the vaguest impression which it has once recorded? In my dreams, that night, the two sinister shapes of the Campagna passed before me again, with threatening looks like harbingers of evil. I woke, and they were gone —I laughed at them. These disturbers of my peace clung to me, nevertheless, dogging my steps in the form of a recurrent nightmare. Often, that winter, I saw them — at Cairo, at Luxor, at Damascus, at Constantinople; whenever, for any cause, my sleep was oppressed, the oppression always resolved itself into that prospect of the wide and desolate Campagna, with the same grim peasant figures moving toward me in the gathering twilight. They never spoke, they threatened only with their eyes.

Gradually the visitations became more infrequent, less vivid; and they might have ceased altogether, fading even from my remembrance, but for the accident of my return to Rome, where, in the spring, as I journeyed back from the East, my stay was unexpectedly prolonged. So improbable had seemed this change of plan that I had neglected to obtain the address of my good *vetturino*; and an hour after my arrival, as I walked up the Corso, I found that I missed him sorely. Rome was a strange, unfriendly city without his thoughtful assiduities. By what steps could I regain them ? I had taken hardly ten steps more, when lo ! they were

mine again; for the man drove toward me
along the crowded pavement. Upon the instant our pleasant relations were resumed.

These were the early days of April, and I
was to remain until after Easter, which, that
year, fell late. Winter had melted away at a
breath; the grayness was all gone; and under soft white clouds, which only deepened
the blue beyond them, Rome kept holiday,
for the most part, in dazzling sunshine. The
roses were coming on; and when we drove
now over the Campagna, which no longer
was desolate, but gay with nodding wild
flowers, we often started up a lark, whose
flight was only to be traced by the sweetest
of all bird-songs borne far above our heads
straight into the sun's eye. The days passed
all too swiftly, like the song; even though,
recognizing them as rare ones, I clung to each
tenaciously, avoiding my kind, and keeping,
so far as was possible, to myself.

One evening (that of Easter Monday, to
be exact) after my coffee and cognac at the
big café in the Piazza Colonna, much fre-
quented by chattering soldiers, I grew tired
of their noisy argument, and broke away

from it. Having, as usual, dismissed Bianchi at sundown, I was unattached ; on foot, therefore, I made my way into the Via Nazionale. Glancing up, I saw that the stars were obscured, and felt that a shower threatened. I had no umbrella ; but as I carried over my arm a waterproof coat of well-tested infallibility, rain, more or less, would be nothing. A moment later, when I was halfway up the hill within a stone's throw of the theatre, the first drops fell. I stepped aside into a doorway to put on the coat, which was of that sleeveless, enveloping sort known to Anglo-Saxons as an Inverness cape, dark gray in color ; pleasantly inconspicuous, it looked by night, at least, not unlike the loose cloak so often worn by Italian men.

As I stood in shelter, muffling myself about the throat, I started in surprise at seeing what appeared to be my own likeness passing swiftly along on the other side of the way. At home, it is no uncommon thing for the man of average height and figure to be taken for some one else. We are not all, unfortunately, of a type so distinguished as to induce the belief that Nature, after our satisfactory development, destroyed the mould. Yet rarely, at home or abroad, does one, unprompted, detect a close resemblance to himself. This, certainly, was the first accident of the kind in my own experience; and it proved so startling that I shrank from the impression. I watched the man disappear in the uncertain light, and thought of old, uncanny tales with fatal issues. Then I shrugged my shoulders, and, laughing at my own credulity, turned the other way.

Evidently, it was a gala night at the Teatro Nazionale. There were many signs of that besides the highly colored poster announcing a special performance of "Hamlet," with a famous young actor in the title-part. The bait lured me into a demand for any vacant place obtainable. Nothing, absolutely nothing, was the first answer. Stay! One of the *posti distinti* had just been returned by the purchaser at the last moment—far from the stage it was, to be sure, but still worth having, even at the advanced price. I closed the bargain quickly, hurrying on to grope my way with difficulty; for the lights were down, the ghostly revelations upon the platform at Elsinore already in progress. They seemed a long way off, as I settled into my seat, which proved to be in the right-hand curve of the great horse-shoe, directly under the boxes. The proscenium arch slowly detached itself from the gloom, until I saw its principal box on the left of the grand tier, still vacant, elaborately draped with flags and garlands, — the royal box, decked for the King and Queen! The audience, ever on the alert, awaited their arrival with an indifference to the mimic court of Denmark which even the anguish of the Ghost could not dispel. The prevailing restlessness soon infected me, and I congratulated myself upon my point of view, which, though distant, was not unfavorable.

The curtain fell upon the first act tamely enough; the lights went up, making the whole place resplendent; while the row of chairs in the royal box stood out conspicuously, still unoccupied. During the long wait, I observed with a stranger's interest alien details — the shrill hawkers of books and papers, the persistent, sharp-eyed flower-girls, brazen in their assurance. Then came the signal from the stage, the hush of anticipation; and at that moment something struck my shoulder, darting from it into my hand — a little bunch of white flowers, such as the women had been pressing upon us. But this had dropped from one of the boxes surely. I glanced up, and saw in the third tier, almost overhead, a woman's face peering down at me. She drew back, but not before I recognized the fact that our eyes had met before; though when, I failed to recollect. Where could I have encountered those worn, gaunt features; that keen scrutiny which seemed at once to warn and threaten me? "Grim as fate!" I muttered; "they fade early, these Italians!" I had thought precisely this before of the same face, and knew it now. She was my evil spirit of the Campagna, who had passed me by on that chill November afternoon, haunting my dreams long afterward. Then she had worn peasant garb, now she was in lace and jewels: yet there could be no question of identity. It was she, beyond a doubt. I turned from the stage, and, leaning forward in my place, fixed my eyes upon the box from which the flowers had fallen. The lights were down again, however; I strained my muscles until they ached — in vain.

The second act ended, and still royalty did not appear. There was manifest impatience everywhere and a general outward movement for the interval. I followed, mainly to get a better view of that box in the third tier, which now was empty. Going on into the foyer, I stood in ambush there to watch the faces. All were unfamiliar. The fateful presence, having fulfilled its purpose, if such purpose existed, apparently had left the theatre. I looked at the flowers in my hand, and wondered whether they had been dropped by accident, or whether, like the eyes that seemed to guide them, they conveyed some message capable of interpretation into threat or warning.

The sprays of jasmine were still fresh and sweet. The better to slip into an unguarded buttonhole, they were bound to a long, straight twig from which the waxed thread had loosened. As I prepared to re-wind it, a gleam of white underneath resolved itself, upon reversal of the thread, into a narrow strip of paper tightly curled about the twig.

Unrolling this, I found scrawled upon it in pencil these words : —

" He will not come."

This, then, was her message. Though without date or signature, the cramped irregular handwriting had a feminine cast; not for the fraction of an instant could I doubt that it was hers. But the purport of it? Who would not come? What was his coming or not coming to me? Why, of all men, had I been selected at the moment for this covert notification?

I stuffed the flowers and the paper into my pocket, and went back to my place at the sound of the signal-bell, noting by the way that the occupant of the third-tier box had not returned. The act began; and it was well advanced when, suddenly, at a word of command the lights flashed up. At once, the voice of Denmark died away in a broken period, while all action upon the stage came to a standstill. With one impulse the spectators, high and low, rose at the entrance of the Court, which was accomplished swiftly and silently. Almost in the same instant the

Queen was seated in the place of honor, bowing and smiling an acknowledgment of the applause which welcomed her, while the household grouped itself in the background. Then the lights were turned down, the motionless actors woke to life, the tragedy resumed its course.

My republican eyes found in the small ceremonial but one cause for disappointment — the absence of the King. I had assumed, not unnaturally, that he would be there with the others; and I was not the only one to assume it, as much whispered comment about me clearly proved. But the subject was soon dismissed, and the whole house became absorbed in the question of the play, which now swept on superbly into a triumph for its chief interpreter. At the end, following the audience out at leisure, I found the better part of it drawn up in the halls and corridors as if for a supplementary pageant. What ceremony else? I wondered, and was not long in doubt. Down the wide sweep of staircase, which seemed built for the purpose, came the Court, preceded by footmen in scarlet livery; there was a glitter of gold

lace, a rustle of silken fabrics, a gleaming of
jewels, while the crowd looked on in solemn
silence, with heads uncovered. All eyes were
bent upon the Queen's face, which now was
sad and preoccupied, deepening by its look
the reverence they paid. I stood at the foot
of the stairs, and could have touched her as
she passed. This unlooked-for epilogue, at
once so stately and so simple, impressed me
profoundly. Yet it oppressed me, too ; when
it was over, and the last carriage had driven
off, I breathed more freely. Graceful as the
expression of faith in the people had been,
I doubted its worth in view of the attendant
risk. In these perilous days of death-dealing
inventive power, of fanatical crimes committed in the name of liberty, was it well wholly
to unhedge the King of his divinity and
leave humanity unbridled ?

"After all, the King was not there," I
argued, as I walked to my hotel through
the drenched, deserted streets; " he did not
come." A weak, inconsequent conclusion,
yet it haunted me all the way like a refrain,
and, seated by the fire, I found myself reit-
erating it. "He did not come." The bit of

staircase etiquette with its dangerous possibilities had given me a new sensation, which
stood foremost in my thoughts. By way of
diverting them, I pulled out the crushed
flowers, the enigmatic message which read
now like the echo of my own persistent bur-
den. "He will not come, — he did not
come!" Were the two one and the same?
Was it the King to whom the woman's word
had reference? For the moment I seemed to
have solved the riddle. But why should she
desire to furnish me — a stranger— with that
information? Why, unless she mistook me
for some one else? No; I must still be wide of
the mark, for that was inconceivable; such
a mistake would imply a very close resemblance; surely, in Rome I had no double —

The thought, the word, brought me to my
feet with a sharp cry. No double? I had
one, and had seen him three hours ago, —
there in the Via Nazionale, a few steps from
the theatre. What if my seat there had been
his, but just relinquished? What if through
a coincidence, strange, indeed, yet not impossible, I, his counterpart, had acquired and
occupied it? Admitting this, the woman's

error was the most natural thing in the world. Moreover, this would explain, as nothing else could, her interest in me at our former meeting upon the Campagna. It had amounted almost to a recognition. She had been on the very point of speaking, and her changed purpose held in it a wonder ill-concealed. Why? Because it was my fortune or misfortune to be the living image of a man whom she knew well, whose presence at the theatre to-night she had confidently expected.

The more I thought of it, the more convinced I became that in this resemblance lay the clue to the enigma. But when, striving to follow the clue, I sought a definite solution, I was soon lost in pure conjecture. That my double in some way had gained in advance the information conveyed to me, and so absented himself from his post, was not improbable. But to what did the information tend? to whom refer? That it involved the King I had really not the smallest proof. I was, perhaps, merely entangled in the meshes of some vulgar intrigue, — some rendezvous, frustrated or postponed.

The next morning, for once, the faithful Bianchi failed me. When his hour came, I received word that he was kept at home by a slight cold, and that I might expect him on the morrow, if the day were fine. Perfect as that was otherwise, it brought no sign of him; and fearing that he might be seriously ill, I went as soon as possible to his address in the Trastevere, which, this time, I had been careful to procure.

The street was a dark, narrow one, between the river and the Janiculan Hill. I found the house without difficulty, amid a long row of dingy tenements. The cabman's rooms were at the top, up innumerable stairs. He lay in bed, restless and feverish, attended by his wife, a shy, gentle soul, prematurely old. The place was neat, but poorly furnished. On one bare, whitewashed wall hung a colored print of the Madonna; on another, a crucifix above a shelf filled with tawdry ornaments. The woman, agitated by my visit, nervously dusted the one chair in the room, and, after drawing it for me to the bedside, fluttered away.

Bianchi was much distressed at the thought

of putting me to inconvenience. He had
tried to come, but the doctor's order prevented that; and so he had written me a letter by the hand of his grandson. It was
somewhere about — on the shelf, perhaps.
I did my best to quiet him, begging him not
to talk ; then, as he insisted, to relieve his
mind I looked for the letter, which lay, as
he supposed, upon the shelf behind me. In
taking it down I accidentally overturned a
small unframed photograph that stood against
a vase which held a spray of artificial flowers ; and when I picked up the card to re-
place it, I could scarcely suppress a startled
cry. For the portrait, taken from life, was
of the woman — my sibyl of the Campagna
and the Teatro Nazionale — who had disturbed repeatedly my waking hours and my
dreams.

After a second look, to make sure, — as if
the face were one that I could forget ! — I
put back the photograph, and a few moments
later went away without gratifying or even
betraying my curiosity concerning it. I had
questions to ask, but poor Bianchi was in no
state to answer them, and I let them all await

his convalescence or recovery. Fortunately, for my peace of mind, I did not have to wait long. His malady with timely care was soon checked; in a week he was on his box again. Then, catching him in a confidential mood on one of our long drives together, I soon discovered the surprising fact that the woman was none other than his own daughter. She had been well married in her own class to a skilled workman of the quarter; had borne him one child, the grandson, Hector, now an inmate of Bianchi's house; but, developing ambitious tastes above her station, she had followed false standards which she was pleased to call advanced, — secretly, at first, until detection precipitated an end that from the first was inevitable. Then she had left all abruptly — home, husband, child — for a rich man, whose creature she had become. He was a brute, a barbarian, a social outcast, a skeptic, irreconcilable, irresponsible; he had cast his evil eye upon her, and had enticed her away. It was believed that they were in foreign parts; just where, no one knew. The husband had died; Bianchi had taken the boy to bring him up; but as for the woman, once his daughter, he disowned her, — she was dead to him. It was his wife, poor, tender-hearted soul, who clung to that likeness of her, which he longed to tear into a thousand pieces. If the signore understood! Santo nome di diavolo!

His story trailed off into a storm of oaths that grew inarticulate with tearless rage. I had no heart to torment him further by any detail of my own adventure. It could avail nothing to state upon the best of evidence that his degenerate daughter was a little nearer than he imagined. I let all go, and lapsed back into silence, while my good friend's wrath slowly wore itself out. We were coming in from the Valle dell' Inferno, and at the Ponte Molle, where the ways diverged, I chose the Flaminian one, for a turn in the Villa Borghese.

It was a perfect Roman afternoon. The old elms of the Villa avenues were in full leaf; the wide, grassy slopes gleamed with daisies, violets, and anemones; the students of the Propaganda, in particolored gowns, played ball sedately on their green amphitheatre, around which a double line of carriages circled back and forth in continuous parade. All ranks were represented, all nationalities. We were democratic and informal. Yet we could be formal, too, upon occasion; for when the Queen came by in state, we straightened in our seats and doffed our hats to her. And when the King followed, not in state at all, but driving, himself, in a high dogcart with an officer at his side, we did the same for him, even more punctiliously, if possible. Then we drove on among the moss-grown fountains, the gray marbles, the clumps of ilex, the long vistas of sun and shade; until, meeting royalty again in another segment of the circle, we looked the opposite way, according to etiquette, in the proud consciousness of duty done — as if such exalted personages could recall our humble features and the fact that we had paid our tribute loyally.

We passed the Queen for the second time with averted faces, and the King drew near. Close before him in the advancing line came a low, one-horse victoria of no richer appointments than our own. Almost abreast of us its horse reared and balked, — plunged,

reared again, refused to go on. Instantly a
space opened beside us, while all beyond stood
still. The King's way was blocked; general
confusion threatened; there were contradict-
ory shouts, which only confirmed the brute
in his obstinacy; and the man on the box
seemed to have lost control of him. The
stolid fellow, with his hat pushed over his
eyes to shield them from the setting sun,
clutched the reins mechanically, incompe-
tently. Bianchi hesitated for a moment. Then
he pulled up the Moor, handed me the reins,
and made a dash for the bridle of the unruly
horse; he caught it, dragged him down, was
dragged along in his turn almost to the
ground. The victoria swept past me with its
occupants, a man and a woman whom I
scarcely noticed, until the man leaped down
almost at our wheel and disappeared among
the carriages. But not before I had a good
look at his face — a startled look it must have
been; for I recognized in him my double of
the Via Nazionale.

Bianchi had conquered. I glanced behind
and saw that the horse was quieted. The victoria drove on without hindrance, smoothly

enough. But as it passed my *vetturino*, he saw
the woman, and a change came over him.
His genial face grew white with anger, then
flushed to the temples. "*Canaglia!*" he hissed;
and, turning after her, repeated with a shout
the obnoxious word, "*Canaglia!*" She paid
no heed to it — was gone. In rage ungovernable he stamped and spit upon the ground;
then, recovering himself, he rushed back,
climbed to his box, seized the reins, and started
forward without a word. The woman was
veiled, as I remembered, and I had caught
the merest glimpse of her; yet I suspected
instantly who she was; before I could con-
firm the suspicion, however, a stir in front
of us diverted my thought. I heard a scuffle
in the crowd, a murmur of excitement. The
King passed again, driving as before, unruf-
fled, at the accustomed gait. A stern voice
ordered us to move on quickly. As we obeyed,
whirling by to join the fast receding line at
its vanishing point, I saw a man, with his back
toward me, led away by the police, and understood that within a few feet of us, for some
indeterminate offence, an arrest had been
made.

What had happened? We wondered and demanded on all sides, but no one could enlighten us. When, fifteen minutes later, we returned to the scene of our adventure, the crowd had dispersed, the carriages were few and far between. Impending twilight marked the limit of the fashionable hour, and we turned the Moor's head toward home. Bianchi's low spirits were apparent; but I forbore to question him, until, as we crossed the Piazza del Popolo alone in the dim light, he gave me a sidelong look so mournful that it appealed for sympathy. Leaning forward, I whispered, "It was she, then!" And he, through his clenched teeth, replied: "Yes, signore. Here in Rome, *la malcreata!* Oh, the shame of it!" with an amazing sequence of muttered imprecations. I let him alone; but, later, at the hotel door, shook his hand and tried to cheer him — wasting my words, for he would not be comforted.

The mystery of the arrest was cleared up in the next morning's paper, where I read of a bold attempt to assassinate the King in the Villa Borghese. During a momentary halt in the line, a man had sprung — from the

earth, as it seemed—to the carriage-step
with a drawn knife in his hand. Providen-
tially, at that instant the King's horses had
started up; the man's foot had slipped; and,
falling, he had been easily disarmed, captured,
dragged away to prison. There he bore himself with unexampled indifference, impli-
cating no one else, refusing to explain his
motive, or to make any statement whatever,
beyond the simple fact that he was an Englishman; a fact doubted by the authorities.
Then followed a rough woodcut of the pris-
oner, who was described as well dressed and
sufficiently presentable in appearance. The
sketch hardly warranted even this craftily
qualified clause about his looks. Yet with its
help I promptly identified my enigmatic
shadow—run to earth, at last. The resemblance, now reduced to its lowest terms, was
most unflattering. But I could only attribute
that to the draughtsman's lack of skill, and
rejoice that things were no worse—or no
better.

Nothing in the printed report connected
the assailant with the blockade in the line
of carriages. The whole affair had been of

a moment only; and the man, worming his
way in and out between the wheels, might
well have seemed to spring from the earth.
But for his familiar face, he would have
slipped by me unnoticed. Now I perceived
plainly that, in his deep-laid scheme to gain
a sure foothold and possible escape, the halt
and the small distraction occasioned by it were
important factors. He had reckoned confidently upon both; but he had reckoned without Bianchi. Through the *vetturino's* quick
wit and ready resource, unconsciously working to a purpose unforeseen, the scheme had
miscarried. Thus did my spurred imagination, so long ineffective, suddenly begin to
patch these shadowy proofs together into one
clear, substantial whole.

Nor did imagination stop there. Its vivid
light streamed backward, making significant
my adventure at the theatre. The abortive
attempt in the Villa Borghese seemed to me
no sudden impulse, but the outcome of a deliberate plot, an organized conspiracy, in
which several minds had long been actively
engaged. The woman, surely, must be an
accomplice; so, likewise, the too incompetent

driver of the victoria, who might or might not have been her former companion, the dull-eyed spectre of the Campagna. Intent upon the King's murder, they had awaited a favorable opportunity, which almost offered itself on that gala night in the Teatro Nazionale. Had the King attended the performance their attempt would have been made at its close, as he walked down the staircase, within reach of the assassin's hand. But something had occurred to change his plan, and word of the change had been passed on to me, in mistake. The deed of yesterday proved the tardy *dénouement* to which these threads had tended.

For an hour or so I contemplated a descent upon the police, to put myself and all my theories at their disposal. But sober second thought reversed this rash intention. The ways of the police were inscrutable. My testimony, as I foresaw, would involve me in awkward not to say vexatious delays, conflicting with all my plans and of most unpleasant publicity; when all was done, it might well be deemed too slight and lead to nothing. The plot, if plot there were, had failed completely, yielding the law its victim. Here was a conclusion upon which I could rest comfortably. It was clear that in Bianchi's mind the two incidents of the halt and the attack were unrelated. He had not seen his daughter again; he neither knew nor wished to know her whereabouts; she had passed beyond the pale of his conjecture even. There I resolved to leave her. And when I said farewell to him and Rome a few days afterward, nothing had occurred to shake my resolution.

At the moment of departure, as a matter of course, I had tossed a *soldo* into the Fountain of Trevi to insure my return, but with small faith in this traveler's charm, which, indeed, failed to work for many a day. Ten years and more elapsed. Then, through a happy whirl of Fortune's wheel, I found myself in Rome once more, with a whole month —the month of May—before me. Again, almost my first thought was of Bianchi. But, this time, no sudden stroke of good luck conjured him up. I had kept his old address, and wrote to him there, receiving no answer.

I watched for him in the Corso, inspected cabstands, questioned porters, without result. At mention of his name all shook their heads. And, finally, I dropped the matter.

A Sunday came which was to be my last in Rome. As I returned on foot from St. Peter's, in the afternoon, through the Via Condotti, the declining sunlight shone full upon the distant church of Santa Trinità de' Monti rising above the vista of the Spanish Steps against a clear blue sky. I remembered opportunely that this was the hour for the fine choral service there, at which, on Sunday, the nuns of the adjoining convent assisted. Hurrying on, I was still in time for a portion of the office; and pushing aside the leathern curtain, I went in.

The dim nave was crowded to the intersecting grate which defends the nuns and their sanctuary from the world. Through the bars, afar off, gleamed the candles of the altar, the vestments, the swinging censers; the unseen choir sang, the organ boomed, the smoke curled upward in the encroaching darkness. I listened to the music, idly watching the beam of daylight that stretched across

the nearer pavement when the curtain swung
inward. Suddenly, revealed for the moment
in its glow, stood the figure of an elderly
man, shabbily dressed, broken with years and
with illness too, perhaps, for his gait was uncertain. He limped forward into the shadow,
and became immediately absorbed in his de-
votions. The picturesqueness of the man and
his reverent attitude interested me, and I
studied his face, which now was but just
discernible. "He is a little like Bianchi," I
thought; "though much older." Then, remembering that I had not seen my former
friend for ten years, I began to wonder
whether it could be he. "No, impossible!"
I soon decided; yet I drew toward him for
a better and more searching look. Just then,
in the distance, came the benediction, and
the man knelt slowly and painfully. Turning his head for an instant, he caught my
eye, but with no light of recognition. "It is
not he!" I sighed.

None the less, when, a few moments later,
the man rose, and, after dusting his knees carefully, moved toward the door, I followed him
out, down the steps at his own slow pace,

keeping close behind him. As he reached
the piazza, he turned with an air of mild
surprise. "Is your name Bianchi Andrea?"
I asked.

At the sound of my voice he started,
flashed upon me the old sparkling look, and
knew me instantly. "Dio mio, Dio mio,
Dio mio!" he chattered, like a parrot; "what
a combination, what a combination, caro
signore! To think you should be there in
the church! It was the Madonna that led
me to it!"

"Bianchi! It is really you! Still at your
old trade!"

"Of course!" he laughed, limping toward
the *vettura*, which stood near by. "See!
Here is my horse. Alas, no longer the Moor!
But what a combination! Dio mio, Dio mio,
Dio mio!"

"You have been ill? You are lame."

"Naturally, since I am old. It is nothing.
My health is not so bad."

"And your wife? She is well, too?"

"Ah, signore mio! She is dead,—dead
these two years. Yet I am not alone; the
boy is with me, and—"

At that moment we were interrupted by the *vetturino's* fare for the time being — two elderly women, severe in aspect, evidently English and single. They had followed from the church, and now eyed us with impatient wonder. I could do no more than give Bianchi my address, bidding him come to me on the morrow. He clambered to the box and drove off; while I, left alone, slowly recovered from my astonishment at this happy chance which had reëstablished the old relationship — with the Madonna's help, as I, too, was half inclined to believe.

We made the most of the two days left me, with many a blessing for the belated favor. When the end drew near, I told him that I must see his grandson before going away, and begged him to drive at once to his lodging. It was not the old place, but a brighter and better one in a new quarter. My visit had been timed for the breakfast hour, when the youth, who was a laborer, would not fail to be at home. In a few moments he appeared, stalwart and unabashed — a tall, manly fellow, who looked as if, upon occasion, he might prove as valiant as his namesake, the Trojan hero. While we talked together, a voice summoned him, and he excused himself. The meal was ready, he had a sharp appetite. "Con permesso!" And he went out.

His keen, black eyes recalled others, still unforgotten, that I am not likely to forget. Upon my lips trembled a question, which I had been often tempted to ask during the previous forty-eight hours. Yet the subject was one that I wished to make Bianchi, himself, introduce, if that could be accomplished. He may have read my thought; for while he shifted his position uneasily, his eyes avoided mine. "Let us go!" I said; and he sprang eagerly toward the door; but at the sound of a step on the landing outside, he drew back, as a woman stood before him in the doorway. Pale, worn, wasted by disease, in dress of the humblest sort, she would have been unrecognizable but for the eyes, which, shining with what now seemed unnatural brightness, betrayed her identity even through the transforming mask of years. She recoiled at sight of us; then with a murmured apology for her intrusion, shuffled hastily away.

An inner door closed behind her. And when all was quiet, Bianchi silently led the way out. Not until we were in the open air did he meet my inquiring glance. Then there was no need of further question. At once he told me the little there was to tell, readily and volubly.

After that chance encounter in the Villa Borghese, his daughter did not cross his path again, and he heard nothing of her for a long time. All trace seemed lost forever. But his wife upon her death-bed, convinced that the daughter was still alive, had exacted from him a promise that if any appeal should be made, he would hearken to it. His wife died and was buried. Then, three months later, word came that his daughter had returned to Rome ill, if not dying, and in want. He had kept his promise faithfully, going to her relief, cancelling all the past, and bringing her home to die, as he believed. She was there; she had recovered, in a measure; but there was no harm in her now, as one might see at a glance. She devoted herself to her boy, to him, to her mother's memory. Oh, an angel of devotion ! What would the signore have? It had been a sad story, but it was well over. In this world, one must be a good father or one was nothing.

Upon that word we parted company. And it is the last word of his that I remember. Our leave-taking of the next morning at the station, hurried and formal as it was, slips wholly from my recollection. The honest-hearted fellow turned back into the Roman streets, where still, perhaps, grown older and grayer, he pursues his calling. If so, at church, or Corso, or piazza, with the Madonna's help, we shall surely meet again. If not:

" Atque in perpetuum, frater, ave atque, vale ! "

THE END

www.ingramcontent.com/pod-product-compliance
Lightning Source LLC
Chambersburg PA
CBHW022207010726
47493CB00002B/445